MIDNIGHT RAINBOW

Recent Titles by Donna Baker from Severn House

A MAN POSSESSED
SOME DAY I'LL FIND YOU

MIDNIGHT RAINBOW

Donna Baker

This first world edition published in Great Britain 1998 by
SEVERN HOUSE PUBLISHERS LTD of
9–15 High Street, Sutton, Surrey SM1 1DF.
This title first published in the U.S.A. 1998 by
SEVERN HOUSE PUBLISHERS INC of
595 Madison Avenue, New York, N.Y. 10022.

Copyright © 1998 by Donna Baker.

British Library Cataloguing in Publication Data

Baker,   Donna
   Midnight Rainbow
   1.   Iceland – Fiction
   2.   Love stories
   I.   Title
   823.9'14 [F]

   ISBN 0 7278 5306 6

All situations in this publication are fictitious and
any resemblance to living persons is purely coincidental.

Typeset by Palimpsest Book Production Ltd,
Polmont, Stirlingshire, Scotland.
Printed and bound in Great Britain by
MPG Books Ltd, Bodmin, Cornwall.

Author's Note

This story was written before the dramatic eruption that occurred in this part of Iceland in 1996/7.

Chapter One

There was a cheerful bustle about the little airport at Reykjavik as Tara came through with her luggage. She looked hesitantly at the small crowd waiting to greet friends and relatives. Would Jon Magnusson be there to meet her himself? Or – more likely – would he have sent someone else, just to show her how important he was?

"He's a bit of a chauvinist," Mike had warned her. "New Man hasn't made it to Iceland yet, even if they do have a woman president. You might have a tough time with him, Tara."

Tara had tossed her head scornfully. "I can handle chauvinism. You don't spend six months on a South Atlantic survey without learning how to get along with men. There were only two of us girls, remember."

"So how did you handle it?" Mike looked fascinated. "You've never talked about that side of it, Tara. Did you insist on proper respect being paid to femininity, or did you just sink without trace and become one of the boys? Two of the boys, I mean."

Tara threw him a withering glance. "You talk as if those are the only two alternatives. There are other ways of coping, Mike, but I don't have time to discuss them now. Just rest assured that Jon Magnusson doesn't frighten me at all. And there's no reason why he should."

"Unless he realises what you're really up to," Mike murmured, and then gave her his old familiar grin. "But

1

like you say, Tara my love, you'll handle it. I've never known anything yet you couldn't handle. I just wish I was coming to Iceland with you, to see you handle Jon Magnusson!"

Well, that was something no one was going to see, Tara thought now, as she scanned the faces at the barrier. Handling – touching of any kind – was definitely out. Using her femininity to get her own way wasn't Tara's style at all; she preferred to succeed on her own merits. And romance was definitely not on her agenda.

Particularly as far as Jon Magnusson was concerned. She'd heard too much about him. She felt she knew him already from the letters he had written to her confirming their arrangements. She certainly knew his type. Brash, arrogant, conceited. That would be Jon Magnusson. Too important to come and meet her himself – he'd said he would send someone else. And as hostile towards her as she felt towards him, simply because she was a woman . . .

"Tara Hansen? Over here!"

Tara looked round quickly. A tall man, head and shoulders above the rest of the crowd, was brandishing a sign with her name on it. Presumably this was the emissary Jon Magnusson had sent to meet her. She gazed at him, impressed. With that height and build, he could well have been one of the original Vikings. She could just imagine him at the helm of a longship, steering by the stars, exploring where no man had ventured before, perhaps one of the first to discover America itself . . . Maybe this trip was going to be fun after all. But he wasn't coming all the way, she remembered with a sigh. Perhaps Jon Magnusson didn't like the competition!

She reached his side and looked up, meeting eyes as blue as the northern seas, and felt her heart give an odd little twist. For a brief moment, they stared at each other and then the moment was gone. The Viking reached out and took her suitcase from her hand. She let it go as if in a dream, then shook her head and dragged herself back to earth. What on earth had happened to all her resolutions?

"Good flight?" His voice was laconic as he uttered words too banal for Vikings, but before Tara could answer he was striding away across the arrivals hall. Hitching up her backpack, she followed him, almost running to keep up with his long stride. Didn't he realise she was at least a foot shorter than he and not equipped with seven-league boots?

"What's the hurry?" she panted, catching up with him at the glass doors. "We don't have a train to catch, do we?"

He glanced down at her, unamused. "There are no trains in Iceland. Didn't you know that?" There was a flicker of scorn in his voice and Tara felt her face burn. Of course she'd known that – she'd been to Iceland before, after all. But before she could retort, he was off again and there was nothing she could do but follow.

Well, she was beginning to revise her opinion of this man already! Tall and fantastically good-looking he might be, but that evidently didn't stop him being as arrogant as the original Vikings he resembled so closely. Maybe it even made him worse. Handsome men always seemed to be the most conceited, and why she'd allowed herself to be impressed even for a moment, she couldn't imagine. He hadn't even had the courtesy to introduce himself. Tarred with the same brush as his boss, obviously!

And why should she run after him like this anyway? If he was so rude and thoughtless that he couldn't be bothered to wait for her, let him get ahead and lose her. He'd be the one in trouble if anything went wrong, after all. Deliberately, she slowed down and dawdled, and sure enough she could soon see only his fire-gold head above the rest of the crowd. When he turned, he'd have lost sight of her completely, and she giggled a little. Serve him right!

Her amusement turned to irritation, however, when the departing crowds thinned and she could see no sign of her escort. Where *was* he, for heaven's sake? Surely he hadn't just abandoned her? And she felt the first twinge of fear when she realised that he'd gone off with her suitcase. Had he come from Jon Magnusson at all? Had he just been some opportunist adventurer, out to rob her – or maybe worse?

But he knew my name, she argued with herself. He knew I'd be on that flight. And then she reminded herself that it hadn't been any secret that she was coming to Iceland. The University of Iceland had arranged for Jon Magnusson to liaise with her and he'd probably mentioned it to people he knew. But it still didn't make sense for anyone to meet her simply to make off with her luggage! Unless – unless there had been some other motive.

Suppose someone had got wind of what she was doing for Mike Redland? Suppose someone wanted to find out more about that – maybe prevent her from carrying out her task? Perhaps the Viking had even meant to kidnap her . . .

Tara shook herself again. Really, she was letting her imagination run away with her. There was no reason at all why anyone should want to do such a thing. But she supposed that she'd have to find someone to help her now, reluctant though she was to ask. Being stranded without luggage at Reykjavik airport wasn't at all the way she'd meant to start.

As she hesitated on the tarmac a large car drew up beside her. Tara jumped back nervously as the door opened, and then her anxiety vanished, to be replaced by fury as the Viking himself stepped out.

"Where have you been?" she demanded, her voice high with anger. "I thought you'd abandoned me. Don't you realise everyone else has gone? I've been all alone here—"

"Well, you poor little girl," he drawled, and she felt an additional rage at the amusement that quivered in his voice. "Frightened, were you? It is pretty late, I agree, but nothing was likely to happen to you. This isn't London, you know."

"I wasn't frightened!" she snapped. "Though you obviously wouldn't have cared if I had been. I just didn't know where you'd gone."

"Well, you know now. I went to fetch the car. And you very sensibly waited here for me – just as I expected."

Tara gasped. "As you'd *expected*? But you couldn't have known—"

"What else could you have done? And," he pointed out smoothly, "you did, didn't you? So now why don't we stop arguing and get in the car? There's a nice comfortable hotel bed waiting for you – and another one for me. And I don't know about you, but I'd rather like to get into mine as soon as possible."

Tara stood irresolute for a moment, then shrugged. What else could she do, after all? Maybe she had over-reacted, and if she told him of the fears that had chased through her mind while she stood waiting, he would either laugh at her or decide she was crazy.

"I suppose you realise you'd have been in trouble if anything had happened to me," she said coldly, getting into the car.

He lifted shaggy eyebrows. "Trouble? With whom?"

"With Jon Magnusson, of course," she said impatiently. "I don't suppose he'd be too pleased if you went back and told him you'd lost me, would he?"

The Viking stared at her. Then he shook his head slowly. "I don't suppose he would," he said, but there was a note in his voice that sounded infuriatingly as if he was trying not to laugh at her and Tara felt her annoyance increase further.

Oh, bother the man – he really wasn't worth talking to! Obviously full of conceit, he probably looked on her as nothing but a brainless bimbo and a waste of his precious time. And if this was an example of the sort of man Jon Magnusson sent on his errands . . .

Jon Magnusson . . . the name had been in her mind for

5

some time now, ever since she had first heard it in Alec's office. Even then it had struck her as one not to be trifled with, and if he were in authority over this man, this Viking at her side, he must really be something. Because this was no wimp, she thought, no man to take orders from anyone he didn't respect. But then, weren't all Icelanders like that? Made tough, independent, uncompromising by the very nature of the land they lived in?

She glanced out as they drove away from the airport and into the city. The lights of Reykjavik sparkled in the clear night air and automatically she glanced up to see if there was any sign of the Northern Lights, a sight she loved and never tired of. But perhaps the city lights were too bright, for even the stars were pale. Still, no doubt the Lights would be visible on other nights. She had never visited Iceland yet without at least one brilliant display.

She glanced at the man beside her. He drove positively but without aggression, which surprised her – she would have expected him to be the kind of driver who believed the road was his. He kept his eyes firmly ahead, making smooth gear-changes that barely altered the note of the engine. His hands were light on the wheel and she found her eyes lingering on the long fingers, noting the gleam of blond hairs on his wrist.

At once, she jerked her gaze away. What on earth had got into her? She'd met attractive men before and managed not to let them impress her – especially when they'd proved themselves as rude and domineering as this man. So why, when she had already made up her mind that she disliked him, was she letting this man get to her?

Well, at least she wouldn't be bothered by him for long. When they arrived at the hotel, he would presumably hand her over to his boss and disappear. And anyway, once she'd met Jon Magnusson, she'd have other things to worry about.

Like how to carry out the task Mike had given her without arousing his suspicions . . .

And that's not going to be so easy, she thought as they drew up in front of the hotel. From all I've heard, Jon Magnusson is sharper than the average needle and will be watching me like a hawk. That's if he's interested in what I'm doing at all – he might well just consider the whole thing beneath him.

Whatever his attitude, she didn't think he was going to be easy to deal with. But then she shook herself impatiently. What was he, after all, but just another man?

The Viking was out of the car and taking her case and backpack from the boot while she was still struggling with the door. As he glanced round and came to help her, she got the door unlocked at last and scrambled out. Feeling tired and irritable, she followed him into the hotel.

He went straight to the desk and by the time she reached him he had given the receptionist her name and been handed her key. Waving aside her protest, he set off towards the lift with her bags and Tara followed, not sorry to have his help. Exhaustion was now washing over her in great waves and all she could think about was lying down and resting her head on a soft pillow.

All the same, she could have done without the lift being quite so small. What with her luggage and the Viking's size, there wasn't much room for Tara as well, and she found herself squashed into a corner, far closer to his big body than she liked, and sharply aware of his nearness, the male scent of him, the warmth of his breath.

She glanced up at him and looked away again quickly as she found his eyes on her, cool as an arctic sky. Her face burning, she stared at the floor, but when she risked another glance he had turned his head away and was examining the walls of the lift. All the same, she was almost sure there was a twitch of amusement tugging at his lips and her colour rose again. Was he laughing at her? And what was so funny anyway?

She would be thankful to be rid of this irritating man and meet his boss, the great Jon Magnusson himself. Not that he'd be any better, she thought, as the lift stopped. In fact, she was beginning to wonder if Iceland was full of men who thought they were still living in the age of the Vikings!

Alone in her room at last, she unzipped her suitcase and pulled out the few things she would need for the night. She washed quickly, then rolled into the wide bed, snapped out the light and closed her eyes thankfully.

But sleep, which she had expected to fell her like a blow, did not come. Instead, she found her mind suddenly awake, scurrying about like an ant. The sound of the aircraft's engines sounded in her ears once more. The bustle of Reykjavik airport was all about her. And she was looking again into those cold, arctic eyes . . .

No! She would *not* allow him to destroy her sleep. She turned over, trying to get comfortable. There was nothing wrong with the bed, it was her own tension that was making her muscles ache, the tension of over-tiredness and disappointment. Yet what had she to be disappointed about? What was this silly feeling that somehow she'd started on the wrong foot, that nothing was going to go just as she'd planned?

Tara thought back to the evening when she'd met Alec MacDonald at the party held to celebrate her parents' thirtieth wedding anniversary. Alec was an old friend of her father's. They'd known each other as students at Edinburgh University, though Alec had switched quite early on from being a medic. All those bodies had put him off, he said, and he'd gone into teaching instead. But now he'd left that too and was setting up a holiday agency.

"Beach holidays in Spain?" Tara had asked him teasingly and he shook his head.

"Something different. The sort of holiday that gives you more than a few days roasting yourself in the sun – gives you something to remember. *Experience* holidays." He stopped and gazed at her, his eyes suddenly bright. "That's it! That's the name I've been looking for. Experience Holidays. Or maybe Tours – would that sound better, d'you think? Experience Tours . . . hmmm."

Tara brought him gently back to earth. "They both sound wonderful. But tell me what you plan to do. What sort of experiences are you offering?"

Alec blinked. "What sort of experiences are there? Whatever's different, off-beat, exciting, fascinating. Searching for lost civilisations in Peru, meeting penguins in the Antarctic – you could help me there, Tara – discovering truth in Thailand . . . There's no end to what could be done. You see, I believe that a holiday should be more than just a couple of weeks doing nothing – though sometimes that's needed, I admit. But most people would benefit more from a *real* change. Seeing a different way of life, learning about a different culture, getting a glimpse of the rest of the world. They'd come back really refreshed, their horizons widened, with new ideas, new knowledge—" He stopped and grinned. "Sorry, still can't help being a teacher, after all these years."

"It sounds fascinating." Tara gazed at him, feeling his excitement move in her own veins. "There are all sorts of different themes you could explore. History, archaeology—"

"Religion. There's a growing interest in the Eastern religions, like Buddhism. Why not take groups of people to see where it all began?" His eyes had begun to glitter. "Tara, you're inspiring me! Talking to you is making it all take shape. The beginnings of things . . . the beginning of civilisation, of thought, the beginning of the world . . ."

Tara laughed. "Now you're talking geology! Why not throw in a few volcanoes as well? A bit of living history. Iceland, for example: the youngest country in the world, still being formed. Volcanoes, glaciers, hot springs, geysers, brand new islands being thrown up in the sea—"

"And only two hours away by air." Alec stared at her. "Tara, you've got a brain almost as brilliant as mine! Now listen – didn't your father tell me you've nothing in view at the moment? No exciting new expedition on the horizon?"

Tara shook her head. "After a year in the Antarctic, I feel I need a holiday myself. But I'll have to find something soon. Lecturing or something, I suppose, though that seems terribly dull after—"

"Then why not join me?" Alec's eyes gleamed behind their spectacles. "Help me get this venture off the ground? I'm going to need people who are experts in their field, who can reconnoitre the countries I want to visit, seek out their possibilities, set up ideas for an itinerary. Bright young people like you, with lots of energy, who understand what it's all about. People with no ties – you haven't any ties at the moment, have you, Tara?"

"No." She shook her head, feeling a sudden emptiness. Yet she thought she'd got over all that . . . Maybe it would be a good idea to get away for a while after all. She looked at Alec doubtfully, not quite sure how seriously he meant this sudden offer. "Do you mean it, Alec? I don't know much about ancient civilisations—"

"But you know about geology. You got a First, didn't you? You've done quite a bit of travelling, too – New Zealand, now there's a place we could look at. The Antarctic – well, I'd have to think about that a bit. And Iceland. That *is* a place we could explore – literally. Near enough not to be too expensive, interesting enough to be a good start. Yes, I think we could really do something there."

"But what would you expect me to do?" Tara was

beginning to catch his excitement. "What kind of holiday are you thinking of, Alec?"

"The kind that's relevant to the country," he said positively. "As I said, ancient civilisations in South America, religions in the Far East, the beginning of the world in Iceland, where it's still happening. Geology, Tara. Holidays that will take people to the best sites, the most interesting volcanoes and glaciers . . . Oh, you know more about it than I do. *You* think about it and then come and give me some ideas." He looked around the crowded room. "We can't talk properly here," he said in an irritated tone, as if Tara's parents were being deliberately unhelpful in inviting so many people to their party. "Come and have lunch with me tomorrow and we'll thrash out a few ideas then."

Lying in bed in Reykjavik, Tara smiled to herself. She could not remember ever having actually agreed to Alec's proposals. But his excitement had been infectious and at lunch next day she'd found herself with the job of coming to Iceland and working on a number of ideas for a geological study tour that would match all his claims for an Experience Holiday – the name he'd finally settled on for his agency.

It had been just what she needed after the rigours of the Antarctic: something that used her knowledge yet made no harsh demands on her and gave her rather more comfort than she'd been accustomed to lately. Living in a hut or a tent in snow and ice had lost its appeal for the time being, she thought, and the idea of a real bed to come back to every night had definite attractions.

"All right," she'd told Alec as they finished their lunch that day. "I'll do it. I'll go to Iceland, anyway, and if that works out I'll think of some other places you could use and do the same thing there. It's an interesting idea and I'd like to see it work. There are plenty of people who'd enjoy that kind of holiday, I'm sure."

"Well, of course, there *are* similar ideas operating already,"

11

Alec admitted. "I'm not exactly first in the field. All the same, I think I can offer a little more – something just that bit different from the rest. And if I can recruit a few more enthusiastic youngsters like you, Tara – well, I'll be home and dry."

Tara grinned. At twenty-six, she didn't consider herself exactly a 'youngster'. But her enthusiasm was certainly blossoming, and by the time she went home that afternoon her mind was already whirling with ideas.

The only smudge on the horizon had been Mike Redland.

Mike Redland hadn't always been a smudge on Tara's horizon. Indeed, it wasn't so long since he'd been the horizon itself – if not the whole of her world. Ever since that first day at university when she'd been searching for her room and feeling very lost and unsure of herself, Mike had been there to guide her, to advise her and set her right.

Or so it had seemed at the time. And Tara had been glad of his help. The campus was overrun with people older and more confident than herself, absorbed in their own affairs and with little time to spare for a fresher who couldn't even remember the way to her own room. But Mike had seen her wandering aimlessly about the corridors and had taken the trouble to stop and find out what was wrong. And then he'd not only shown her the way, he'd taken her there and then invited her to come out for a coffee with him. And from that moment on, they'd been inseparable.

Tara could see now that she'd depended on Mike too much in those early days. As the youngest in her family, she'd always had someone to turn to and, much though she wanted to be independent, the first few weeks at university surrounded by strangers could easily have overwhelmed her if it hadn't been for Mike. But he had taken the place of her brothers, and by the time she had found her feet and felt more ready to cope for herself, she was in love with him.

Or thought she was. Looking back, she could see that early passion as an immature love, little more than a testing of the water. A bubbly, lighthearted affair that should have been enjoyed for what it was and never taken seriously. And maybe that was how it would have stayed, if it hadn't been for Mike's own expectations – and problems. And the effect they had on Tara herself.

When had the balance of their relationship changed? she wondered. When had she stopped being the dependent one? When had Mike stopped being the one in charge? Not that he would ever have admitted as much. Even at the end, he'd considered himself the decisive one, accusing her of not knowing her own mind, of being a quitter, of being selfish . . . But Tara knew herself well enough by then to ignore his taunts. And when she was away from him, thousands of miles away in the Antarctic, with plenty of time to think, she'd seen quite clearly that for a long time she had been carrying the burden of their relationship – the burden of Mike himself.

But she'd never quite realised it – until the day when she'd told him about the Antarctic expedition.

"A *year*?" Mike had repeated when she met him, bubbling over with the news. "You're not going to go?"

"Of course I am!" Surprised, she'd stared at him. "It's a terrific chance, Mike. I can't let something like that go by. I'll be able to study glaciology, the effects of erosion on the coastline – everything I'm interested in."

"But what about me? What am I going to do?"

"What you're doing now, I suppose. Unless you want to try something different too. It's up to you."

"You don't care, do you?" he accused her. "You're so full of this, you haven't even given me – *us* – a thought. You're just going to go swanning off to the other end of the world and you haven't even stopped to wonder how I'm going to manage without you. I don't suppose the idea even entered

13

your head." He turned and stamped away to the other end of the room.

Tara started after him, then paused. Mike was right. She hadn't wondered what he would do without her.

"I suppose I thought you were adult enough not to need me around all the time," she said to his back. "I suppose I thought you were as capable of finding opportunities as I am. Mike, don't you think you're behaving a bit like a spoilt child?"

"Oh, that's right, put me in the wrong. I've just got to stay at home being faithful while you go and live in the middle of nowhere with a lot of other men." He turned and stared at her. "Are there any other women going on this expedition, Tara? Or is that a silly question?"

"There's one other," Tara answered. "And yes, it is a silly question." She went towards him. "Mike, a year isn't all that long. And we're not officially engaged. You've never seemed to want to be tied down. Maybe we need some time apart, to figure out just what we do want." She held out her hands. "Come on, don't let's quarrel over this. If it was you going I'd be thrilled for you."

"That's easy to say," he muttered, but he came and took her hands, looking earnestly down into her face. "Tara, is this some way of telling me you're fed up with me? Or that you're tired of being 'just friends'? If you want to get engaged, I'd be—"

"No," she'd interrupted quickly, knowing that was just what she didn't want. "No, Mike, I don't want you to offer to marry me just to keep me here. That wouldn't be the right thing to do at all. Look, let's have this year apart and then think again. Maybe we'll find we really can't live without each other – and then we'll know what to do, won't we?"

Mike had agreed then. But over the next few months, as the plans for the expedition gradually took over Tara's life, he withdrew into himself. He'd been quiet, depressed, so that

14

in the end she'd given up telling him about the expedition and begun to feel guilty that she was going. At one point, she'd even considered backing out, but she knew that if she did she would regret it for the rest of her life. And she knew even then that he had been trying every way he could think of to prevent her from going.

Their last evening together had been a disaster. Tara had been unable to conceal her excitement, but at the same time was racked with guilt and already half aware of a simmering resentment that she should feel guilty at all. Mike didn't own her! He'd always known she wanted to do this kind of thing. He couldn't possibly expect her to be ready to stay at home with her knitting, not at only twenty-three years old. But she couldn't say so. She could only do her best to comfort and reassure him.

"The year will be gone like a flash. You've got interesting things to do as well. I'll be back in no time at all."

"You'll be back in a year. That isn't 'no time'. And who's to say what can happen in a year?" He stared at her. "You're going to be down there all alone with twenty men—"

"Not all alone. Cathy'll be there too."

"Oh, big deal! What a chaperone she's going to make, with twenty guys milling around. Men get very lonely, you know. They need women – and with only two of you between twenty—" He shook his head. "The whole thing's crazy."

"We're not going as comforts," Tara said coldly. "You talk as if Cathy and I are going to be shared out as a sort of after-dinner treat. We're geologists in our own right and we have our own projects to complete—"

"Yeah, yeah," he interrupted rudely. "And you're not taking your biology with you, are you! You're not going to think about sex at all. You're going to put it all on ice for a whole year. Pull the other one, Tara!"

Tara bit her lip, then reached out and put her hand on

15

his arm. "Mike, don't let's quarrel. This is our last evening. Let's make it a memory we'll be happy to have for the rest of the year."

He turned then and took her roughly in his arms. "Tara, I'm sorry. I didn't mean any of those things. It's just that – oh, I'm going to miss you so much. And I'm scared . . ."

"Scared of what?" she asked gently. "There's nothing to be afraid of, Mike. I'm not going to fall for anyone else."

It was only later that she'd realised that that wasn't what he was afraid of. Even then, Mike had known that he couldn't stay faithful for a whole year. Perhaps he'd even known who he was going to turn to. Perhaps he'd known that he just wouldn't be available any more when Tara returned.

Tara had set off next day only half reassured by their parting. But her worries had faded as she became caught up in the excitement of the expedition, the flight to Buenos Aires, the voyage to the Arctic Circle and the overland trip to the research station. Out there in the wilderness of ice and snow and rock, England had seemed like a different world, and when she thought of Mike it was as if she saw him down the wrong end of a telescope.

Only their letters made him real. And over the months, his grew more and more remote. She took them out into the harsh brilliance of the sunshine and read them surrounded by inquisitive penguins, trying to understand what lay behind the terse phrases. Was it the loneliness he had feared, or was there something else?

And when the year was over at last and she returned, excited to be going home but sad to leave the wild beauty of the icy desert, she was already dreading what she would find.

She knew the truth the moment she saw Mike's face, that first evening.

He hadn't wanted to tell her. He'd stepped forward and

kissed her cheek. Her *cheek* – when he should have been sweeping her into his arms and almost smothering her with his passion. And then, with only the briefest of looks into her eyes, he'd turned away again, taking her luggage.

Nevertheless, brief as it had been, that one look had been enough.

"Mike." She caught his arm. "*Mike*. Wait a minute. Please."

"I'm looking for a taxi. We'll never get one in this scrum—" He was actually trying to shake her off! Tara felt the tears come to her eyes. She was exhausted after the long flight and yearning for a real welcome, the sort that would tell her she'd been missed, that she was still loved. A spontaneous hug and shower of kisses that would set her own fears firmly at rest.

"Mike—" But this was neither the place nor the time to start a deep discussion. He had found a taxi and was already hauling her luggage aboard. She scrambled in and collapsed on the seat beside him, almost too tired to speak. She waited for him to put his arm around her and hold her close, perhaps kiss her again, but he did nothing. He simply sat beside her, looking straight ahead and talking to the driver.

"I've booked into a little place near Paddington," he said. "I didn't think you'd want to go too far tonight."

"No. Thanks." We're talking like strangers, she thought. And what has he booked? One room or two? She felt a bubble of hysteria rise inside her. She had no idea what Mike was expecting, what he was planning. Suddenly, he really was a stranger.

The taxi pulled up outside a small hotel and Mike paid the driver and dragged her luggage out. Together, they climbed the short flight of steps and entered the small foyer. It was clean and bright, and the receptionist welcomed them warmly. But Tara was too weary to do more than nod when she was told her room number, and allow Mike to take the key and open the door for her. They went inside and he set her cases down and looked at her.

"I hope this is all right. I hope you'll be comfortable here."

"Yes." Tara looked around. It could have been a hotel room anywhere. Two beds, a built-in wardrobe, a long shelf with a mirror above, a kettle and two cups and saucers. A small bathroom. Clean, adequate and impersonal. Totally unsuited to a lovers' reunion – but if they'd really been lovers, she thought sadly, it wouldn't have mattered where they were.

Mike was fidgeting awkwardly, not meeting her eyes. He made a half-hearted move towards the door. "Well – if you've got everything you want—"

Tara put out her hand. "Mike—"

"Yes?" He sounded bright, artificial, and he still wasn't meeting her eyes.

"Mike, what is it? What's wrong?"

"Did I say anything was wrong?"

Tara shook her head. "You don't have to. It's obvious. You've hardly looked at me – you haven't even kissed me properly. Mike, I've been away for a whole year—"

"By your own wish," he cut in. "*I* never wanted you to go. You know that."

Tara stared at him. Were they just going to start again from where they left off? Pick up the pieces of their quarrel as if the year between had never happened?

"All right," she said, trying to keep her voice steady. "It was by my own wish. I've never denied that. I always wanted to go on a trip to the Antarctic, and now I've been and I'm glad I went. I think it was worthwhile; I've done some useful work. But—"

"But now you expect to come waltzing back and find everything just as you left it – including me." He was angry now – the anger, she suspected, of a man who feels guilty and resents it. "Well, life isn't like that, Tara. It doesn't stand still. You can't go swanning off to the other end of the earth for a year and expect everything to stay just the same. I'm sorry, but there it is."

He stood looking angry and stubborn, like a small boy who is trying to justify his naughtiness. Tara gazed at him and felt a sudden surge of pity. She went forward and laid her hands on his arms, looking up into his face.

"Mike. Mike, don't look so unhappy. I know I left you on your own, but – well, it was something I'd always wanted to do. I didn't want it to change things between us."

"Well, it has," he muttered. "I told you it would, and it has." He made another move towards the door. "Let's talk about this some other time. I'll ring you at home—"

"No!" Tara gripped his arms. Exhaustion washed over her in waves, and she longed to collapse on one of the beds and sleep, but she couldn't let Mike go like this, with so much unexplained." Mike, you can't just leave me. You must tell me – what's happened? What's gone wrong? I know I went away, but I'm back now and we can be together. We can start again—"

"We can't." His voice was brusque. He stared down at her and she saw the hardness in his eyes, the clench of his jaw. "It's over, Tara. I'd have told you months ago, but it wasn't easy when you were so far away." He felt in his pocket and pulled out an envelope with her name on. "Look, I've written you a letter, I thought it would be better. It explains everything. Read it tomorrow, when you're not so tired."

Tara stared at the envelope. Then she looked up at him. A numbness crept over her limbs, crawled all the way over her body. When she spoke again, her voice was flat.

"No, Mike. We've had enough letters over the past year. Just tell me." And when he still didn't speak, she drew in a ragged breath and said quietly, "You've found someone else, haven't you?"

He nodded.

"Someone I know?"

"Her name's Heather," he said. "I met her three months after you left. We were just friends at first, then it grew into something more." He looked into her eyes at last, pleading. "I never meant it to happen, Tara. But I just couldn't help it. I missed you so much, I was so lonely, and she was *there*. And then I realised I was falling in love with her." He shot her another look. "We're getting married."

"Oh," Tara said blankly. "I see." She stood quite still for a few moments, waiting for the numbness to pass and the pain to begin, but nothing happened. After a minute or two, she said, "When? When are you getting married?"

"Next month. On the fourteenth." He looked at her again. "I'm sorry, Tara. I really am. But – I did try to warn you. It's not my fault."

"No, of course not." She felt quite detached. "I'm sorry, too, Mike. For asking too much of you." For a few more moments she stayed quiet, then stepped away and said brightly, "Well, there we are then. And thanks for all you've done – coming to meet me and finding me this room." She looked around at the impersonal walls, the two neat beds. "I'll be fine here. All I need is a place to sleep, after all."

"Tara, I'm sorry—"

"It's quite all right," she said, still in that bright voice. "Don't worry about it at all."

"We'll still be friends. It won't make any difference to that."

"Oh, no. No difference at all."

"Heather would like to meet you."

"Would she?" Tara asked, genuinely surprised. "Would she really?"

"Yes. She wants to – to explain about it. You see, she didn't know – I didn't tell her—" He was looking guilty again, and the self-justification crept back into his voice. "Well, why should I? We weren't engaged. So she didn't set out to steal me or anything, and she doesn't want you to think—"

"Oh, I don't. I don't think that at all. Tell her I quite understand." Tara wished he would go. They'd said enough. Now she just wanted to be alone.

"So will it be all right? We'll be friends – the three of us?"

"Yes. Yes, of course. We'll be friends." Tara felt she would have promised anything at that moment, just to get rid of him. She patted his arm. "I'll even come to your wedding, if it will make you and Heather happier. Just let me know what you'd like for a wedding present. And now – I'm sorry, Mike, but I'll have to ask you to go. I really do need just to sleep."

"Yes, of course." He bent and gave her the most genuine kiss he had managed yet. "Tara, you're an angel. I just wish—" He shook his head sadly. "I just wish things could have been different."

And I just wish you'd go, Tara thought, feeling that if she tried to speak she would scream. Instead, she smiled again and pushed him gently towards the door, and this time, to her immense relief, he went. The door closed behind him and she was alone at last. She stood for a moment, looking round the room. Bare and empty. That's life from now on, she thought.

Too tired to unpack, even to wash, she slid out of her clothes and lay down on one of the beds, waiting for the pain to begin.

Thinking back to that time now, Tara realised that the pain had never really begun. Exhaustion had overcome her that

21

night, and she had known nothing more until she'd woken ten hours later, wondering for a moment where she was. And then there'd been just too much to do. She'd gathered herself together and set off once again, this time for her parents' home. There had been work to do on her project, meetings to attend, papers to be written up. Life had been so busy for a while that she'd barely had time to think about Mike.

She'd met Heather, surprised to find her so glamorous, and attended their wedding as a gesture of defiance against those who might have suspected a broken heart. Let Mike Redland and his cronies think he'd broken her heart? Never! And that had been her guideline all through the months that followed. Nobody was to see that he'd hurt her. She would not even admit it to herself. And as the months slipped by, she buried her feelings, pretending they weren't there. It seemed to be the best way, and the best way to avoid being hurt again was not to let anyone else come as close to her as Mike Redland had been.

I'm better alone, she thought. I'm strong – stronger than Mike. I can live without a man. Mike had proved that he couldn't live without a woman, but it didn't have to be Tara. It probably didn't even have to be Heather. He just needed someone to relate to, someone who would let him control her, someone he could show off, control, manipulate – someone who, like a mirror, he could look at and see himself. To prove he was real.

Poor Mike, she thought with compassion, catching a sudden glimpse of the insecurity and fears which must seethe within him. How sad, to have to go through life depending on other people to make you feel real. And how sad for those you have to control, who lose sight of their own lives in the process.

And how thankful she was to have escaped . . .

But now here she was in Iceland, still being manipulated by him. Still having to twist her own life in order to do what

22

Mike Redland wanted, even though he was now married to someone else, even though he had no power at all over her. Why was she doing it? Why did she let him use her like this? Tossing in her bed, she remembered that day back in Glasgow when Mike had asked her to visit him.

She'd gone somewhat cautiously, not sure what he wanted from her now. He and Heather were married, after all, and back from what had obviously been a very successful honeymoon. She'd seen them once or twice, Heather smiling complacently and Mike smoothly pleased with himself. She wasn't sure she could bear any more of their almost blatant delight in each other. After all, there'd been a time when she and Mike . . .

Still, Mike had been insistent and eventually she had agreed to go. Once at the house he and Heather had bought, she had been whisked straight upstairs to Mike's study, where his new computer had been installed and where he was busy working through some program he had written for it.

"What's all this about, Mike?" Tara felt uncomfortable, alone here in his study with him. Heather hadn't seemed to mind, had almost urged her to follow him upstairs while she went back into the kitchen, but all the same . . . "I don't think I ought to stay too long."

"Rubbish. You'll have a meal with us. Heather's expecting you – she's cooking up something delicious right now." Mike closed the door. "You know we look on you as a special friend, Tara."

Wonderful, she thought, since at one time I thought you looked on me as something more . . . But there was no sense in going back over that now. She'd made the first move away, after all, when she'd elected to go on the Antarctic expedition. Maybe Mike had been right when he'd told her she wouldn't have done it if she'd really cared about him. Or at least not been so cheerful, so excited about it. Maybe

23

they wouldn't have got married even if she had stayed. Or if they had, maybe it would have been a disaster . . . She caught her thoughts and stopped them firmly. Hadn't she convinced herself it was no use going over all that, time and again? It was over and she wasn't broken-hearted after all, just determined not to let any man get to her so deeply again – so perhaps it really was all for the best.

"So," she asked again, "just what is this all about, Mike?"

He moved towards the computer and pressed a couple of keys. "I want you to look at this."

Tara glanced at the screen. It was producing a column of figures but they meant nothing to her. She looked at them more closely and shook her head.

"What is it?"

"It's a model." He was staring intently at it. "A projection. Look, Tara, they denote the incidence of volcanic eruptions in various parts of the world. Hawaii, Japan, Asia. See how they follow a pattern? If these figures, this interpretation of them, had been available years ago, quite a lot of the later eruptions could have been predicted with a fair degree of accuracy. Do you see?" He ran through several tables, explaining his calculations. Tara watched and listened, absorbed and fascinated, her doubts forgotten. Mike had really got something here, she thought.

"So what you're saying is that by using these projections, you can pinpoint the next eruption in any particular area?"

"That's right. Place and time. Approximately, of course, but it's getting more accurate all the time." He looked at her. "You realise what this means, don't you?"

"Lives could be saved," she said, beginning to understand his excitement. "Towns under threat could be evacuated. Perhaps we could even control the flow of lava, stop it destroying so much land, if we only knew in time when and where it was likely to appear."

Mike nodded and moved quickly on through the program. "That's right. Though in most places, the threat is pretty well known and monitored already. Most of these countries know where there's danger and when it's likely to appear simply from past experience, which is, after all, only a less sophisticated version of this method. But now let's look at Iceland."

Tara stared at the screen. Mike had moved into graphics now, a profile of Iceland's mountains with symbols of explosions to denote eruptions. They were all there: the great eruption of Hekla in 1783, the emergence of the island of Surtsey in 1963, the eruption that had almost destroyed Heimaey in 1974. And others, eruptions that hadn't happened yet, eruptions his program suggested would happen in the future.

Most of them were more or less where they might be expected. Hekla again. Others in the north. And then . . .

"But there's never been an eruption there!" Tara said. "What makes you think—"

"Look at the figures. They follow a pattern, you see?" Mike ran back over the program and showed her again the pattern that had emerged. "That one there – then this one a few years later – this, this and finally – *this*." He watched the explosion on the screen, then turned to her. "See what I mean?"

Tara stared at it, disturbed. "A new fissure volcano! But that would mean— Mike, there are people living there. Farms. A village. A town."

"That's right," he said. "And if my calculations are correct, they're right in its path."

"But they ought to be warned!" she exclaimed. "There might be something they can do—"

"To avert a volcano? Come on, Tara, you know it's impossible. We're not talking damming rivers here. This is fire, lava, magma – and nobody knows how much there is, boiling away down there."

"So they'll have to evacuate." In her mind's eye she could already see the terror, the panic, as the earth opened up in a series of craters, each one belching fire and molten rock. But Icelanders didn't panic easily. Look at what had happened on Heimaey, the cool, efficient way in which the entire island had been evacuated without a single fatality. "If they have enough warning, they could move everything – rebuild."

"If they have enough warning, yes. And there is time. It's not going to happen next week or even next month. Maybe not even next year. But happen it will, Tara. All I have to do is convince them."

"Convince them? But surely when they see these figures—"

"If they'll look at them, yes." He hesitated, then said reluctantly, "I just don't think they'll pay any attention."

"But why not?"

"Because they come from me," he said flatly. "And I've crossed swords with one or two people in Iceland. No need to go into details but I just don't think they'd give my ideas much credence. I need some on the spot research – a few tests made – to back them up."

"And that," Tara said, beginning to understand, "is what you want me to do."

He grinned at her. "Just spy out the land a bit. Obviously you can't take the equipment needed for proper tests. But you can have a look around. I'll tell you the spots I think need investigation. And then you can report back to me and we'll try to do something more conclusive. Once I've got real proof, they'll have to listen."

Tara had thought they would listen anyway. Any country as unstable as Iceland had to allow for the unexpected. But eventually she had agreed to do as he asked.

"You're marvellous, Tara," he'd exulted when she had finally given in. "And don't forget, there'll be a spot of credit in this when it's known. I shan't forget your part in it."

Tara shrugged. She wasn't much interested in credit. Her main concern was that the people who lived in the path of the new volcano – if it really was a danger – should be warned.

All she had to do was make sure that Jon Magnusson didn't find out what she was doing. Because Mike had impressed upon her that Jon was his arch enemy. Not only would he dismiss the whole thing, but if she did manage to convince him, he'd claim the credit for himself. "He's just that sort," Mike had told her. "Don't trust him an inch, Tara. He's as slippery as a snake and just about as reliable."

They went downstairs and into the living room. It was large and brightly lit, furnished in what Heather said was 'minimalism' – in other words, Tara thought, not very much. The coffee table and the few chairs there were seemed to be made of nothing more than spindly steel tubes and black plastic or leather; there was one scarlet rug on the polished wooden floor and a huge picture on one wall which appeared to be a representation of water disappearing down a plug hole, in shades of swirling blue. A steel trolley stood in one corner, with a few bottles and glasses set out on it, and there was one bookcase which bore a leather-bound set of the works of Jane Austen, not, Tara thought, what one would have expected Mike to choose, so presumably they were Heather's.

"Good heavens," she said faintly, seeking wildly for something nice to say. "What a – a striking room."

"It is, isn't it," Heather said proudly. "I got the idea when I was in Scandinavia. I spent quite a lot of time there, you know – Norway, Denmark, Sweden. They all furnish their houses this way."

"Do they?" Tara wasn't sure this was true. She wondered how many Scandinavian homes Heather had actually visited. She sat down gingerly on one of the steel and plastic chairs and accepted the drink Mike was holding out to her.

27

"Oh yes." Heather sat opposite. She wore black leggings and a gold, scoop-necked top which was so understated it must have cost a bomb, and she was festooned with gold chains. "Didn't Mike tell you? My father does a lot of business there. A bit like the one you're working for, I suppose, but a lot bigger of course. He's in charge of the design side."

"Oh." Tara looked down into her glass. Although she'd tried hard to make friends with Heather, she never felt at ease with her. Probably that was inevitable, when one considered that the other girl had virtually stolen Tara's fiance behind her back – though, as Mike had been quick to point out, they'd never been formally engaged – but Tara had made up her mind from the start that she was going to deal with this situation in a civilised manner. No recriminations, no possessiveness or jealousy. So, after that first shock Mike had dealt almost as soon as she'd arrived back from the Antarctic, she had smiled sweetly, congratulated him and Heather, and gone shopping for a wedding present. She'd gone to the church and watched them stand together at the altar, and toasted their happiness afterwards with that same smile nailed to her face. She hadn't even allowed herself the luxury of slipping away from the reception early, but had stayed to throw confetti as the newly-weds drove off.

And inside, she had ruthlessly thrust her feelings away. She would *not* feel bitter, she told herself fiercely. She would *not* rail against Fate for what had happened. She would not allow *anyone* – least of all Mike and Heather – to know how hurt she felt that he hadn't thought her worth waiting for. That he had never really loved her.

But try as she might, she could never quite bring herself to make friends with the girl Mike had chosen to be his wife. And she knew that Heather felt the same about her. Somehow, even though she had married Mike and might thus be said to have 'won', she always seemed to feel the need to impress.

If only she knew, Tara thought, that it takes a lot more than a few steel and plastic tables and chairs to impress me. Like a squashy sofa and a log fire, and one or two real pictures on the wall . . . But that wouldn't be Heather's style.

She wondered if it was really Mike's. He was standing by the trolley now, holding his glass and looking big and awkward, as if he didn't properly fit into the small room. He caught her eye and gave her the slightly shamefaced smile that indicated he too was uncomfortably aware of the tension.

"So, tell us all about this job you've got," he said, a little too heartily. "Being a holiday rep sounds a bit of a comedown after something as grand as an Antarctic expedition."

So he hasn't forgiven me, Tara thought. Lightly, she said, "Oh, I don't know. It's just a holiday job, after all, so what could be more appropriate? And I'm not exactly a rep – I'm doing a survey, to see what kind of tours Alec will be able to offer."

"Hmm." He sounded thoughtful. "So Alec sees Iceland as the next smart holiday destination, does he? The next place in fashion?"

"I don't think so. He's not interested in fashions. He sees it as a place people who really want to get to know the country will like to visit."

"No pleasure domes, then? No up-market holiday parks with thermal jacuzzis and cable cars over the glaciers?"

"I wouldn't think so for one moment," Tara said, knowing he was goading her and determined not to allow herself to feel nettled. "Alec would run a mile before getting involved in anything of that sort."

Mike shrugged. "It's where the money is."

"I don't think Alec's interested in making money—"

"Of course he is," Mike said sharply. "Everyone's interested in making money. We've all got to eat and have a roof over our heads. Even you – otherwise why would you be bothering with a tinpot little job like this, when you've got the sort of qualifications you've got?"

Tara blinked. Mike's aggression had taken her by surprise. As she remembered him, when they'd been students together he hadn't been bothered all that much about money, had lived in old jeans and eaten baked beans with the rest of them. So what had changed?

She took another look round the room. Flimsy though it looked, this sort of furniture must be expensive. Pictures like the Blue Plug Hole might look as if a child could have done them, but probably fetched huge sums. And all that gold jewellery hanging round Heather's neck hadn't come from Woolworths.

"I've told you," she said quietly, "I'm doing this as a fill-in, while I decide what direction to take next. And as it happens, I don't consider it a tinpot job. I think Alec's doing something worthwhile – making fascinating parts of the world accessible to people who are really interested. Of course he has to make a living – but he's not interested in money for its own sake. And he would never dream of turning a place like Iceland into a theme park."

"He's missing the point, then," Mike said. "Because that's what people really want. Most people, I mean, not the odd few." He turned and poured himself another drink. "He needs to join the real world, Tara. And so do you. A year in the Antarctic seems to have made you forget what life's all about."

Tara stared at him. There was a note almost of bitterness in his voice. "And just what is it all about?" she asked quietly.

There was a moment's silence. Then Heather jumped to her feet and laughed nervously.

"Why ever are we all so serious? This is supposed to be a celebration, remember? Tara's first meal with us in our own home. Mike, darling, you're not looking after our guest. Her glass is empty. Fill it up while I go and see if dinner's ready, there's a lamb." She reached up and kissed him lightly, then disappeared through the door to the kitchen.

Mike gave Tara a half shamefaced, half defensive glance and did as he was told. "Sorry about that. But you probably don't realise exactly how expensive life is. You've been cushioned by grants and funding all along the line. Maybe when you've been doing a real job for a year or two, and making your own way, you'll get a better idea."

Tara considered several replies to this. Grants and funding had never made anyone rich, and any extras and quite a few necessities had come from hard work during university holidays, doing a variety of jobs. If she had any money to spare now – which was very little – it was because she hadn't had any need to spend, or anywhere to spend it, during her time in the Antarctic. Now that she was back, she was renting her own flat and well aware of the cost of living. And she wasn't buying expensive furniture, paintings or gold jewellery.

All these thoughts ran through her mind but she discarded them. What was the use? Mike had asked her here to carry out a task for him, and she would have turned him down flat if there hadn't been people's lives involved. The sooner she could leave, the better.

At that moment Heather called through that supper was ready, and Tara got up with a sigh of relief. Mike ushered her through to the dining room, as sparsely furnished as the living room, with a glass-topped table that left their laps and legs totally revealed. Not much chance of playing footsie here, she thought with an inward giggle.

"So," Mike said, lifting his glass, "here's to Iceland.

31

And I hope you'll be able to do as good a job for me as you do for Alec, Tara. Remember – lives may depend on it."

Tara looked at him. There was an odd note in his voice as he said this, but she could not analyse his expression. In fact, there had been something odd about the entire evening. Something that didn't ring quite true.

It's just the situation, she told herself. Me, and Heather and Mike. That's all.

"I'll do my best," she said. "But remember, it might not be easy to do such an investigation without attracting attention. The Icelanders are very careful about what goes on in their country. A stranger wandering about doing tests is bound to be noticed, and I may not be able to pretend it's all in the cause of bringing tourists who are only interested in geology."

"You'll manage," he said confidently. "Anyway, even earnest geologists like yourself need to take a bit of time off occasionally. You ought to be looking at places where they can unwind, relax. The little fishing village I mentioned – Heklavik – for instance. It's ideal. There's a hotel there, a stretch of sand, a little beach – it's straight out of Enid Blyton. It's right where I think my theories could be proved, but you can use the tourist bit as a cover without any problem."

"Not if I'm only looking at it from a geological angle," she argued. "Anyone who wants to unwind can do so in Reykjavik. They don't need to go to a small village miles from anywhere."

But Mike laughed and shook his head. "Don't keep finding objections, Tara. Remember, this is important. How would you feel if that small village was smothered by an eruption and you could have prevented it? Well, not prevented the eruption, of course, but at least given a warning so that people could get away in time. Isn't that more important than finding pretty sites for amateur rock-grabbers to admire? Or maybe it's the money you're most interested in after all. Maybe you'd be more enthusiastic if I could pay you."

Tara flushed scarlet. "It's not that at all." But she couldn't say just what it was that made her feel uneasy about the whole thing. Maybe it was the idea of deceiving the people whose country she was about to visit, even though it might be 'for their own good' as Mike had said. And who was he, she wondered, to decide what was for an entire country's good? But whichever way she looked at it, she always came back to the same inescapable point. It was about people's lives. And you couldn't argue with that.

She was glad when the meal was finally over and she could take her leave. She departed feeling once again that Mike had managed to manoeuvre her into a situation she wasn't going to enjoy.

Sunshine was streaming into her room when she woke next morning, and she rolled over and gazed out of the hotel window at the coloured roofs of the city. Her sleep had refreshed her, and she felt filled with energy. She sat up and caught sight of the hotel booklet, with a picture of a swimming pool on the cover.

A swim! That was what she wanted to start the day. A quick look at her watch told her that it was still early, and there was plenty of time before breakfast. Swiftly, she leapt out of bed and slipped into the scarlet swimsuit she had brought with her, throwing a white towelling robe around her shoulders as a cover-up.

Tara remembered Icelandic swimming pools from her previous visit. Like everything else in this country, they were kept in a state of pristine cleanliness, and this one was no exception. Shoes were left at the door, and swimmers were required to strip naked and take a thorough shower before entering the pool. There was no privacy – Icelandic women strolled about without false modesty, and the changing area was like a scene from a Roman bath-house, with seating amidst the tropical plants that flourished in the warm atmosphere. It was a pleasant place to come even if you didn't want to swim, Tara thought, remembering the bleakness of municipal swimming pools at home. And the fact that this one was in a hotel made no difference – the public pools were just as attractive.

The pool itself was almost empty, with just a few hotel guests ploughing up and down. Tara slid into the water, finding it almost as warm as a bath, and set off, using a fast crawl, for the far end.

Swimming was her favourite sport. She had learned as a small child and excelled at it during her schooldays, swimming for her county in national championships. She kept up her skills, never losing an opportunity to get into the water, and had missed it sorely during her year in the Antarctic. Driving through the water, she thought with amusement that she'd missed it even more than she'd missed Mike. No wonder their relationship had foundered!

After six lengths she paused for a rest, holding the rail that ran along the edge of the pool. There were only three people in the water now and she watched them idly, admiring the swift, clean strokes of one swimmer in particular. He reached the end and placed his hands on the edge of the pool, swinging himself clear of the water and padding along towards the high diving-board.

What a hunk, she thought, watching the muscles ripple in his back and thighs as he strode away. His skin was lightly tanned, a golden brown that looked as if it were mostly his natural colour, and his hair shone like a burnished crown above it. A kinglike figure, or perhaps a Nordic god. The Icelanders were certainly a handsome, godlike race – every one of them a candidate for Hollywood, and this one more than most.

The man climbed, catlike, up the steps to the highest diving-board and stood for a moment at the top, flexing his muscles slightly as he assessed the water. Tara watched, interested to see him dive. And then he turned his head and look straight down towards her.

The Viking.

Her reaction was immediate. With a swift movement, she curled her legs up beneath her and pressed them hard against the side of the pool, kicking herself both away and under the water. Without waiting to see the dive, she swam almost half the length of the pool before surfacing, then completed the journey with the same fast crawl as she had used before and leapt up the steps. Only when she was standing on the ceramic tiles of the surround did she pause to look back.

The Viking was nowhere in sight. She looked about uncertainly, not knowing whether he had dived or not. Perhaps he was still under water, swimming, but she could see nobody at all in the pool now, either above or below the surface.

Feeling a little foolish, uncertain as to why she had found it so necessary to avoid him, Tara turned away. The idea of getting back into the water was unappealing, but she was reluctant to simply go and get changed without experiencing all the delights of the pool. Instead, she made for the jacuzzi.

Like the main pool, this too was empty, a wide, bubbling well, surrounded by tropical plants. Tara lowered herself into it and sank onto the broad shelf below the surface, sitting waist deep in the surging water. She leaned back and closed her eyes.

"Now there's a sight for a beautiful morning," a deep voice drawled. "A naiad, resting in a woodland pool. Not that we have many woods here in Iceland," he added in a more normal tone.

35

Tara opened her eyes. "I'm sorry?"

"Oh, don't apologise," the Viking said quickly, lowering himself into the pool beside her. "There's nothing to be sorry for at all, as far as I'm concerned. In fact, I'm absolutely delighted."

Tara bit her lip. She hadn't been apologising at all, and he knew it. His dark blue eyes were laughing at her. She glanced away quickly, conscious of the blush which was spreading down from her cheeks into her neck, and slid a little further down into the water.

"We didn't have time to talk last night," he continued. "It's a pity the plane gets in so late – everyone arrives worn out. But I daresay you're feeling a bit more human this morning, after a good night's sleep. I trust you did have a good night's sleep?"

"Yes, thank you," Tara said coldly. He was behaving far too familiarly for her liking, as if they'd known each other for years. Probably thinks that just because he looks like a blend of Robert Redford, Richard Gere and Tom Cruise, every woman he meets will fall at his feet, she thought. Well, here's one who most certainly won't.

All the same, she couldn't deny that he had an effect on her. The temperature of the water seemed to have gone up about ten degrees since he'd entered it, and she was uncomfortably aware of the nearness of his bare limbs to hers. A brief swimsuit, though totally respectable, seemed suddenly far too little to protect her – protect her from *what?* she thought bemusedly – and, worst of all, she had a feeling that he knew exactly what she was thinking. Those dark blue eyes were definitely amused . . .

"Pleasant here, isn't it," he drawled, lying back and letting his long, golden legs drift to the surface. "Can't be many more better ways of starting the day. Well, maybe there's one . . ." He slanted another gleaming look at her.

Tara shifted away abruptly. His toes had very nearly

touched hers, and if they had she thought she would probably have jumped as if she'd been stung. She wanted to get out quickly, to show him that she didn't intend to be trifled with, but her own common sense stopped her. He hadn't done anything, after all, and all this could well be her own imagination.

Anyway, once Jon Magnusson arrived, presumably this man, whoever he was, would disappear. Careful and possessive of their country as Icelanders might be, it surely wouldn't take more than one to keep an eye on her while she was here. This Viking was no more than a temporary minder who thought rather a lot of himself, but would soon be on his way and need never cross her path again.

The water was bubbling around her body. It was like having a massage, she thought, only more intimate and rather more sensual. Like being caressed by a lover . . . She closed her eyes for a moment, and felt her senses swim. When would she be caressed again by a man who loved her? Since coming back from the Antarctic, there had been nothing but those brief, passionless kisses from Mike at the airport. Since then, she'd turned firmly away from any other risk of involvement. Only now did she suddenly feel the loneliness of her life, the emptiness of living without love.

The man beside her stirred and Tara's eyes jerked open. Her brief moment of enlightenment vanished, and the fear flooded back. She kicked herself away from him again and stood up, aware that his eyes were on her body, that she was trembling.

"Going so soon?" he asked lazily, but there was a darkness in his eyes that she didn't understand.

"Yes. I've got a lot to do. Sorting things out for the trip, getting ready to meet Mr Magnusson—" She was babbling, she knew, but she couldn't help it. She saw his eyebrows lift. "He'll be here this morning, I presume?" she went on, trying to keep her voice steady. "I really do need to make a start as soon as possible."

"Oh yes," the Viking said, and once again there was laughter in his eyes. "Oh yes, he'll be here this morning."

Tara turned away. She was acutely conscious of his eyes on her as she walked the length of the pool towards the changing area. Thank goodness he won't be coming on the trip, she thought. I won't have to see him any more. The thought of sharing her space with him – any sort of space, closer than fifty miles or so – was more than she could handle.

Back in her room, she quickly rinsed out her swimsuit and hung it over the shower to dry while she had breakfast. She had almost finished when the telephone rang. She lifted it and listened for a moment.

"Breakfast?" she repeated.

"Why not? You do eat, I take it?"

Yes, but not with you, Tara thought.

"Thank you, but I'd rather wait and meet Mr Magnusson when he arrives," she said coldly. "Do you have any idea when that might be?"

There was amusement in the voice and she felt a twinge of annoyance. "Oh yes," he said. "He's here now as a matter of fact. Looking forward to seeing you."

"Oh." She digested the information. "Well, that's different, I suppose. But it'll take me half an hour—"

"Oh, that's fine. He'll wait." There was a definite chuckle now. "He's not quite ready himself – and I know he wants to look his best for you."

Tara hung up, feeling that once again he'd got her at a disadvantage, yet not sure why. Was he implying that she needed half an hour in which to make sure she looked her best for Jon Magnusson? As if she intended to use her femininity to impress him? She had a good mind to just drag on her oldest jeans and not even bother to comb her hair – that would show him his mistake! But it would also be very rude to Mr Magnusson to do so, and no way to start negotiations over Alec's holiday plans. She had to remember she wasn't here simply on her own account; she had a job to do, which she was being well paid for.

Tara sighed. It had all seemed so easy, so exciting, when she'd discussed it with Alec. Neither of them had envisaged the complications that might be imposed on them by the countries they hoped to offer as holiday areas. Perhaps they'd been too naïve.

Not that Iceland's conditions were at all impossible, or even difficult. They simply wanted to ensure that the visitors would be properly looked after and not taken into dangerous situations, while at the same time taking care of the environment. And since the idea was to visit sites of particular geological interest, where normal holidaymakers might not venture, the authorities had suggested that Tara's first reconnaissance should be accompanied by an Icelandic geologist.

"It probably won't be at all restricting," Alec had said when Tara had voiced her dismay at the idea. "It's really not much more than a formality. He'll just come around with you, see what ideas you have and what you intend, and make any suggestions that might be needed. Point out dangers you hadn't thought of, perhaps, or risks that could be avoided. That's all."

"What dangers? What risks? I have been to Iceland before, you know, several times. I know the whole area pretty well and I don't think I'd be taking anyone into danger."

"No, I know that. But *they* don't. And they don't want people falling down crevasses or into volcanic lakes." Alec gave her a pleading glance. "Look, Tara, I know you feel this is a reflection on your capabilities—"

"I have done quite a lot of field work," Tara broke in. "I do know what dangers can be involved. But—"

"And this Icelandic geologist will appreciate that. Don't worry, I'll see that he knows just how experienced you are. I tell you, Tara, it'll be a formality, nothing more. Look on him as a bit of company. You never know – you might even like him!"

Tara gave him a withering glance and Alec grinned. "I don't intend to fall in love with him, if that's what you mean," she said haughtily, and he laughed outright.

"Of course you don't! I didn't mean to imply any such thing. But most people can be likeable enough, if you approach them with the right attitude. So, no hostility, all right? Remember, this means a lot to me."

Tara hesitated, then smiled at him. "Okay, Alec. I didn't mean to be prickly. I'll let this man tag along and make a few suggestions – I might even take one or two on board, if they're good enough. So long as he doesn't try to pull rank on me. I warn you, I won't have that."

"I don't suppose he will, not for a moment." Alec's tone was peaceable, and Tara had had to be satisfied with that. But all the same, she hadn't liked the idea of what amounted to a supervisor on her misson.

Well, now she was about to meet this man. And she hoped that he would be rather more approachable than his sidekick. She remembered Alec's words: most people were likeable enough, approached with the right attitude. So all she had to do was get her attitude right and hope he was doing the same.

And being on time would be a good start! With a guilty glance at the clock, Tara wriggled into clean jeans and a high-necked white sweater which clung to her slender figure. Her green eyes looked back at her from the mirror and she decided on no make-up other than a flick of pink lipstick. Clean and fresh she would be, but dressed to make an impression – no way. This was business, remember?

The Viking had told her to come along to Room 419, only a few doors along the corridor. Picking up the flat case which held her notes and maps, she left the room and made her way along the corridor, pausing briefly to look out of the big picture window.

Reykjavik lay sparkling in the September sunlight. The white houses, with their neat, square lines and cheerful red, green and blue roofs looked like they'd been made with a child's building blocks. Not beautiful, yet with a certain charm of their own. And beyond them rose the mountains, green and rolling as the hills of Wales or the Lake District. And beyond them, further still, the majestic domes of the volcanoes . . .

Tara felt her heart give a quick skip of excitement. Ever since she had been a small child, she had felt this way about the landscape. While appreciating its present day beauty, she had nevertheless known that there was a deeper significance in the rocks and streams, the cliffs and valleys; she had felt an urge to know how they had been formed, what forces had shaped them, how it had all come about. News of earthquakes or volcanic eruptions had found her glued to the televison and her bedroom windowsill had been a rubble of stones picked up at random to take home and gloat over.

"Tara, for heaven's sake stop collecting stones," her mother would say despairingly, and threaten to throw them out. But Tara had been so distressed at the idea that she'd had to give way, and instead had bought her books on rocks which Tara had pored over for hours. With her brothers, she had tramped for hours along the beach near their home or up mountains, searching for stones and trying to understand the landscape. The activities of her friends, from dolls to dressmaking, had never interested her and as she had entered

41

her teens she'd scorned clothes and make-up, preferring instead to scramble about the cliffs in a pair of jeans.

"You're just not normal," her best friend Katy had accused her one day. "You don't even seem to want a boyfriend. Don't you want to get married one day?"

"I suppose so." Tara had spoken absently, gazing down at the rocks from the cliff where the two girls were sitting. "I just haven't met anyone interesting yet, that's all."

"How would you know?" Katy had spoken scathingly. "You don't even bother to look, if they're not carrying a geological hammer. What is it with you, Tara? Are you scared of people or something?"

Tara had looked at her, startled, as the words struck home. But Katy had noticed a couple of young men she knew on the beach and was standing up waving, her remark forgotten.

But Tara had not forgotten it. She'd pondered it later, wondering if there were some truth in it. *Was* she scared of people? Sheltered by her family of brothers, scarcely ever allowed to assert her own independence, had she somehow retreated into a shell? And if so, how was she going to get out of it?

She'd thought Mike was her answer. And so he had been – up to a point. But no sooner had she begun to gain confidence and emerge from her shell than he'd tried to push her back in again. He hadn't *wanted* her to be strong and assertive, even though he'd wanted to depend on her himself. He hadn't wanted her to live her own life, only his.

"So there you are!" A familiar voice brought her jerking back to the present. "Admiring the view? There's an even better one from my bedroom."

Tara turned and gave the Viking a cold look. "I happen to like this one, thanks all the same. Has Mr Magnusson arrived?"

"Certainly. Didn't I tell you he was looking forward to seeing you?" The blue eyes inspected her and again she was conscious of that half-smile, lurking behind their coolness. "Come on in."

Tara followed him through the door. He held it back for her, then closed it so that she went in ahead of him. She was halfway across the room before she stopped, and then she turned to him with wide, accusing eyes.

"He's not here at all!" Her glance swept round the room again. The small table in the window was laid for breakfast – but only for two. "Just what are you playing at?" she demanded, with a twinge of something between anger and fear. "Just what's going on?"

The Viking leaned against the wall, arms folded, and regarded her quizzically.

"Nothing's going on," he drawled, and she restrained herself with some difficulty from striking him. "I invited you to come to breakfast with Jon Magnusson, and here you are. I told you he was looking forward to seeing you, and so he was. I told you he'd be here – *and so he is.*"

Tara stared at him. The truth slowly dawned, and she wondered bleakly why she hadn't realised it from the start.

"You mean . . . *you're* Jon Magnusson?" she breathed.

"None other." He held out his hand, unsmiling. "Nice to meet you, Tara. Jon Magnusson – at your service . . ."

Chapter Two

Tara looked at the hand Jon Magnusson was holding out. Reluctantly, she put her own into it and gasped a little at the feeling of warmth and strength around her fingers. A kick like a small electric shock ran up her arm and touched her heart, and she withdrew her hand hurriedly.

"But why didn't you tell me?" she asked blankly. "Why did you let me go on thinking – well, thinking you were a – a—"

"Minion?" he supplied ironically. "Tara, I didn't even realise that was what you were thinking – not for quite a while. I thought you knew who I was. In fact, I'm pretty sure I told you, only there was so much noise in the airport, perhaps you didn't hear me. It wasn't for some time that it dawned on me that you didn't know, and by then I was so irritated with you I decided to let you just go on in ignorance. To tell the truth, all I wanted was to get to bed—"

"*You* were irritated?" Tara broke in. "Just what did *you* have to be irritated about? *I* was the one who was irritated. Marching off like that and just abandoning me—"

"Which you engineered yourself. I was quite well aware of what you were doing. You could have kept up with me quite easily, but instead you virtually stopped and let me go on. So I did just that. And you can hardly say I abandoned you; I brought the car right to where you were. It would have served you right if I'd made you come and search the car park!"

Tara sighed with exasperation. She turned away and then felt him at her shoulder.

"Look," he said, "this scrapping won't get us anywhere. We've both got jobs to do and we'll do them more efficiently if we're adult about it. Let's start again, shall we?" He touched her hand and she glanced unwillingly into his face. "I'm Jon Magnusson. Welcome to Iceland."

Presumably he was implying that *she* was the childish one. But there was nothing she could do but agree. With a shrug, she said, "All right. We'll start again."

But how possible that was going to be, she didn't quite know. There was no way they could call back the first impressions they'd made on each other. She cast her mind back to those first few moments, trying to recapture exactly what she'd thought of him, and remembered that she'd been impressed by his looks. What had he thought about her?

Well, he wasn't going to tell her now, that was for sure. He was turning to the breakfast table, set out with cereals, fruit juice and rolls. He poured coffee and indicated that she should sit down, and because there didn't seem to be any alternative, she obeyed.

"Well?" he said. "Isn't it a good view? And it's particularly clear today – you can see Hekla."

"I'd already noticed." She was determined to impress upon him the fact that she knew Iceland well already. "I suppose you watched the eruption?"

"Well, not from here, but yes, I did have a good view. We knew it was going to happen, of course. We monitor the earth tremors beforehand and when they get to two hundred a day we clear the area. It was quite a dramatic eruption." He glanced at her. "You didn't take the opportunity to witness it yourself, I take it?"

"I wasn't able to. I was away."

He smiled maddeningly. "Sunning yourself on some Spanish beach? Well, why not? Winters in Britain aren't

45

what we get here in Iceland but they can still be pretty miserable. I don't blame anyone wanting to run away from them."

I wasn't running away, Tara thought furiously, and I wasn't in Spain, I was in the Antarctic. But why should I tell you that? You let me get the wrong idea about you last night, so now you can have the wrong idea about me. You've already made up your mind anyway.

"Your English is very good," she said politely. "I'd never have known you weren't British, except for a slight twang. In fact, I'd probably have thought you were a Scot."

He helped himself to cornflakes. "That's because I am half one. My mother's a Scot and we've always visited her relatives regularly. And I did a year at Durham University after getting my degree here – not Scotland, I know, but near enough for me to spend a lot of time with my grandparents and uncles and aunts. But most Icelanders speak good English, you'll find."

"I know. I have been here before," she reminded him. "I try to practise my Icelandic when I can, though I'm not very good at it. It's not an easy language to learn."

He laughed. "Full marks to you for trying! Not many people do – more's the pity. It may be difficult, but it's a wonderful language, full of poetry. Hence the Sagas, of course. But it's a good idea to learn a smattering, if you can."

"Well . . ." Tara began, then stopped. Why should she tell him that she knew more than a 'smattering'? In fact, she could carry on quite a lengthy conversation. It was the chatter of a group of people, full of interruptions and half-finished sentences, that she found difficult to cope with.

But Jon was already thinking of something else. With a glance at her briefcase, he lifted one eyebrow and said, "Are you planning a working breakfast?"

"I thought that's what I'd been invited for," Tara said

46

stiffly. "I imagine you don't want to spend too much time on this. It must seem very small beer to you."

"Oh, not at all. The tourist industry has a lot of potential in Iceland; our economy needs it. At the same time, we have to be careful to ensure that it isn't exploited." He finished his cereal and sipped his coffee. "Not that I expected to find myself chaperoning a holiday courier round the country, but I'm contracted to do a certain amount of government work so I agreed to take this on. Otherwise you'd have had a university lecturer or someone like that."

"Holiday courier?" Tara exclaimed indignantly. "Look, you seem to have misunderstood – I'm a qualified geologist, I've taken part in an Antarctic survey, I—"

"You're here to map out a holiday tour," he stated implacably. "In other words, a holiday courier – however impressive your qualifications." His tone indicated clearly that he didn't find them in the least impressive. "Just why are you between jobs anyway?"

Tara opened her mouth and then closed it again. No way was she about to tell him about Mike. After a moment or two she said tightly, "I just felt like a rest, that's all. Is there anything wrong with that?"

"None at all," he said smoothly, "for those who can afford it . . . And now perhaps we can discuss the plan you've suggested. There are one or two points I'd like to go over—"

Tara suppressed her annoyance at his patronising tone and reached for a roll. "Can't we do that later? I'd like to enjoy my breakfast first." She offered the basket of rolls. "There's no hurry, is there? After all, if I can give you a good holiday you'll be more likely to recommend Experience Holidays to whatever authority it is you answer to. So why not just relax and enjoy ourselves?"

She was secretly pleased to see that her attitude had evidently surprised him. Presumably he'd expected her to demand that they start rushing about at once. But Tara had learned to play men at their own game, and if Jon hoped to goad her, he'd be disappointed.

There was a slight pause, then he said stiffly, "As you like. Though I still think we ought to firm up on our agenda. I'm a busy man; I only do a small amount of this kind of work. Most of the time I'm abroad, advising on mineral extraction and that kind of thing."

Tara smiled and poured herself some coffee. Despite his earlier words, Jon Magnusson obviously felt he was too important for this job and resented the time it was taking. Well, that was his problem. She hadn't invited him along, after all.

"How are the plans for the hydro-electric scheme going?" she asked lightly and, when he stared at her, added with a touch of impatience, "The sale to Scotland. I suppose you have heard about it?"

"Of course I have. I'm surprised you have, that's all."

Tara sighed. "Why? Why should that surprise you? I can read, you know, and I don't devote all my time to women's magazines picked up at the hairdresser's."

"No," he said, his glance touching her short black curls, "I don't imagine you do."

Tara gasped. Was he implying that she didn't look as if she ever *went* to a hairdresser?

"My hair's naturally curly," she said defensively. "It has to be kept short or it goes wild. Anyway, it's easier to look after on field trips."

His blue eyes widened. "Did I say something wrong? You've got very nice hair." He glanced at it again, appraisingly. "A lot of women spend a fortune to get their hair to look like yours."

Tara felt half mollified, half humiliated. Leaping in too quickly had always been a fault of hers, and more than one man had told her she was too quick to take offence.

But so often, she knew, she'd merely responded as she'd been expected to, if not manipulated into. It was a trick that particularly annoyed her, that of making some mildly insulting remark and then pretending it had meant nothing, or had only been a joke. And there was nothing one could do about such behaviour, other than refuse to rise to the bait.

You'd think I'd have learned by now, she thought. But it came as a fresh surprise when each new man tried it, and maybe she hadn't expected it of Jon Magnusson.

Or maybe she *was* being too sensitive . . .

"So you know all about the hydro-electric scheme," he said after a moment. "Well, it seems to be going through all right. It makes a new export and that's got to be good."

"Iceland's main commodity after fish and woollens," Tara said lightly. "Heat and power, just coming up out of the ground for free."

Jon smiled. "Well, not quite free. We do have to harness it. But, yes, we are lucky to have all that boiling water simmering away under the ground for the taking."

"One of Iceland's great attractions," Tara said. "A cold country – in winter, anyway – with beautifully warm buildings at little cost, and steaming hot pools to bathe in. Those are the kind of things that will bring people – the things that can't easily be found elsewhere."

"And no doubt some of the hot pools will be on your holiday itinerary," Jon said. "Along with Geysir, the Golden Falls and the Blue Lagoon – all the usual tourist attractions, in fact."

Tara gave him a level glance. She'd already smiled at him twice; that was enough for one breakfast-time.

"Back to square one," she said lightly. "We agreed to discuss that later, remember?"

Jon bowed his head, but there was a gleam in his eye and she had a feeling that he'd summed her up as an adversary. Her heart sank a little. This wasn't what she'd intended, a kind of war between herself and the Icelander. She was supposed to be paving the way for Alec's business, not arousing local antagonism.

If she'd succeeded in annoying him in what amounted to the first two or three hours of their acquaintance, it didn't bode well for the enterprise. Perhaps I ought to ring Alec, she thought miserably, and tell him I'm coming back. Tell him to find someone a bit more tactful . . .

For a moment, she toyed seriously with the idea. And then she remembered her other task here in Iceland – the one Jon Magnusson knew nothing about.

Was Mike right in suggesting he would either reject it or claim credit for himself? Somehow, much as she disliked Jon Magnusson, that wasn't the way she read him. But she couldn't do anything about it. Mike had sworn her to secrecy and Tara wasn't accustomed to breaking her promises.

"So can we have our discussion now?" Jon asked as he finished his coffee. "I take it you're still working on the itinerary you sent me? You still want to visit all those tourist places you listed?"

"This is to be something more than the usual tourist holiday," Tara said. "I thought you understood that, Mr Magnusson."

He raised his brows. "Jon, please. It's our custom to address people by their first names, didn't you know? I thought you'd been here before."

Tara flushed. Of course she'd known that, just as she'd known the other peculiarities of Icelandic names: the fact that they had no actual surnames but simply called sons after their fathers, as Jon was called Magnusson, and daughters after their mothers. So if Jon had any sons they would be called Jonsson . . . She wondered suddenly if he were married. And what sort of woman he would choose for a wife.

"So let's start, shall we?" Jon was asking, and she realised from the impatience in his tone that he must already have asked it at least once. Blushing again, she fumbled for her case and pulled out papers and maps which she spread on the table.

"I want to take people to sites of particular geological interest," she explained. "That isn't hard in Iceland, just about everything is interesting. But we want to explore some of the places the ordinary tourist, flying here for a four-day break or perhaps cycling and camping, wouldn't be so likely to reach. Laki Mountain, for instance—"

"That's a long journey," Jon interrupted, and she nodded.

"Exactly. And too rough for a lot of people to attempt. Most tourists, just interested in sightseeing, would find it tedious crossing those great lava fields. But for people really interested in geology, it's a worthwhile trip."

Jon looked at her map. "You've marked Landmannalaugar too, I see. Another long trip, and pretty bare landscape for most of it."

"I know. But its starkness is so spectacular, like being on the moon." She looked down at the papers spread out before them. "I'd like to take them to the crater lake, and of course to some of the great waterfalls. Gullfoss, Ofaerafoss and so on." She paused and looked up at him. "That's just for starters, of course; there are plenty of other things to weave in with those, including the hot springs. I think we can make some really fascinating trips which will not only introduce people to geology but also interest those who already have some knowledge."

Jon stared down at her and she realised suddenly how close they were standing. His warm breath touched her cheek, and she glimpsed a spark of something deep in his blue eyes. Her own breath caught in her throat and she felt a sudden jolt in her chest as her heart skipped.

For heaven's sake! Whatever was she thinking of, letting

this man get to her? Hadn't she lived cheek by jowl with men equally attractive and remained immune?

Yes, a small voice remarked in her mind, but you were in love with someone else then. Now, there's nothing to stop you falling for someone new . . .

Except that I've made up my mind not to, she retorted sternly. Because look what happened to that love. I don't intend to be caught in *that* little trap again, thank you very much.

She turned away sharply, flicking through the papers as if searching for something, and was relieved when Jon moved aside and she could feel her own space about her again.

"You've got quite an ambitious programme there," he drawled. "Have you taken into account such things as the roughness of the roads, glacier melt, the total difference there is in time taken to cover the distances—"

"Of course I have!" she snapped. "Look, Mr – Jon – I'm not a complete novice, and, as I keep reminding you, I have been to Iceland before. I've been to most of these places and I understand the problems involved. That's why I'm here: to explore in detail, take notes and work out the most feasible programme."

"Getting in as much as possible in a short time," he suggested, and she sighed with exasperation.

"Obviously the kind of people who will be coming on our holidays will want to see as much as possible, but they won't want a flying visit to any of these sites; they'll want to stop, listen to an explanation of what they're looking at and then explore on their own. And I want to make the best possible use of the time, without turning it into a race. It has to be fun as well, we want them to try our other holidays too."

"So what are you planning to do?"

"I've got what I think is a good working plan. I want to

do this as if it were the holiday itself. Then I'll be able to see all the snags, if there are any, and report back to Alec before we get the final schedule drawn up."

"Plans!" he said. "Schedules! Doesn't sound much like a holiday to me."

Tara bit her lip and said nothing. It was obvious that she could keep on repeating herself over and over again without effect. Jon simply wasn't listening. Maybe he thought the whole thing was beneath him. He was a leading geologist himself, after all, as well as a successful mineral consultant with businesses of his own. Why should he have been appointed to be her shadow?

"Just what is your interest in this?" she asked curiously. "This isn't the kind of job you'd normally do, I'm sure. Don't you have more important work to do than follow me about?"

His ice-blue eyes met hers and she wondered if he thought she was being sarcastic. But he answered coolly enough. "I like to think all my work has some importance. I can see that on the face of it, supervising a new holiday agency might seem a bit trivial, but, as you are so keen to impress on me, Tara, yours is no ordinary tourist agency, is it? You're coming here specifically to study geology, and that puts a different aspect on the matter."

"Does it?"

"Yes, it does. We're very careful of our environment here in Iceland. We know just how valuable it is. Being such a young country, in geological terms, we know how much it can tell us about the formation of the world itself. Not to mention the North Atlantic Drift, which can be seen actually happening at Thingvellir. There's nowhere else in the world where that can be seen, and if you're going to bring a lot of amateur geologists tramping about, chipping away at the rocks with their hammers—"

"We're not intending to carry Iceland away in our suit-cases," Tara interrupted. "We'll be bringing responsible people, not vandals."

"And how do you know that?" he demanded. "You'll be bringing anyone who can afford to pay. Are you going to subject them to a vetting of some kind before you let them book? Of course not! You don't know who you'll be bringing, Tara."

She gazed at him helplessly. "But you can't just shut your doors to anyone you think might not be fit to be allowed in. You need the tourist industry, you said so yourself—"

"And we also need to monitor it to make sure it's the tourist industry we need," he told her crisply. "We don't want to end up like Spain, a skyscraper development made up of all the worst elements of Britain—"

"You're being totally unfair! Spain isn't like that. It gives people what they want: sunshine, beaches and the kind of holiday they ask for. Iceland will never appeal to the people who want those things."

"No? You think not? You think nobody will look at our constant hot water, our efficient heating systems, and think of building – what shall we call them – pleasure domes? Go to our swimming pool here in Reykjavik, Tara, and see if the idea doesn't occur to you. Better still, tell me truthfully that it hasn't already."

She met his eyes steadily. He held her look, daring her to glance away, and she knew that if she did he would consider her self-condemned.

"No," she said clearly, "it hasn't occurred to me. Nor to Alec. Those are *not* the kind of holidays we want to promote. Nor do we intend to bring people who will damage your geological sites – we're as well aware of their importance as you are yourself."

"So tell me, if you will," he said, looking back at her maps, "why you have marked the village of Heklavik."

Tara felt her cheeks flame. Involuntarily, she cast a quick, guilty glance at the map, but she knew already that the village was ringed in red, as if it were a site of special importance. She looked up at him and found his eyes, cold as chips from a glacier, watching her face. Noting every blush, she thought, every small change of expression.

"There's nothing of geological importance there," he went on. "Nothing except a rather pretty little bay and a small settlement. And some nice flat areas of sandur, sheltered by the cliffs, which would be ideal for building."

"Building?" she said faintly.

He nodded. "Building. Building, perhaps, a pleasure dome?" He held her eyes for a moment and then added dismissively, "Of course, I realise you've no such plans. It's merely a wild idea of my own. But I'd like to know why you did ring that particular village."

Tara glanced at it, feeling her eyes drawn almost guiltily towards the red circle.

"Why?" she said, her voice trembling slightly. "Well, I don't think there was any particular reason – I just thought it looked a nice place to go. As you say, it's a pretty little bay—"

"So you've been there before?" The question came like a pistol shot, and she jumped.

"No. No, as it happens I haven't been there before, but—"

"So how did you know it's pretty?"

"Well, I – you just said so. I—"

"But I've *only just* said so," he reminded her. "And you circled that name before you came to Iceland. So what did you know about it? What plans do you have for Heklavik, Tara?"

Tara gazed at him. She cast wildly about in her mind for some reply that would satisfy him, but could think of none. If only she could tell him the truth! But Mike had

55

impressed upon her the need for caution, especially where
Jon Magnusson was concerned.

'And don't on any account mention my name,' he'd
warned her. 'Magnusson and I have crossed each other in
the past. Never mind how, it's a long story and as far as I'm
concerned, it's history. But he's a man to bear grudges and
if he finds out you know me – well, it won't just be all up
with this—' he'd indicated the computer screen they'd been
watching, '—but your friend Alec's plans will be dished too.
So take my advice and be careful when you're around Jon
Magnusson.'

Tara had looked at him doubtfully, wondering if he might
be exaggerating. But now, seeing Jon's suspicion, she began
to revise her opinion. The blue eyes were as cold as the
Icelandic sea, and even the tawny gold of his hair could not
soften the lines of his face. She was reminded once again
of her first impression of him: a Viking, setting out on a
raid. And likely to – what was it they did? – go berserk at
any moment. The thought of Jon Magnusson going berserk
made her shiver.

"I'm waiting," he reminded her, and there was now a chill
of menace in his tone. "You must have had some reason for
encircling that name."

If only she could tell him! Surely it was something
he'd want to know – that everyone in the village would
want to know. But once again, Mike's warnings came into
her mind.

'They won't believe you. They'll want proof, and while
you're getting it for them, you might as well be getting it for
me. You see, Tara, this is all new, and it could be a big thing
for me.' He'd gazed at her earnestly, his eyes wide with the
little-boy look that she knew so well. 'Nobody's going to
come to any harm, Tara,' he'd said quietly. 'But – well, I
really would like to be the one to tell the world . . .'

She'd hesitated and then promised. And here she was, on

her first morning in Iceland, trying desperately to think of some plausible reason why she had circled the name of that village on her map!

"It's not what you think," she said. "It's just that I – I know someone who lives there. That's all. Someone I met on a field trip once. I – I thought I might get a chance to look them up."

"Them?" His eyes remained fixed on hers, like gimlets boring into her brain. Could he actually *see* that she was lying? Or would her behaviour tell him that, the way she was flushing, the way she was twining her fingers together?

"My – my friend, yes," she stammered, wishing she'd never got into this. Why *had* she marked the map? It had been a crazy thing to do; she might have known that Jon would see it.

"Friend? Or friends?" he persisted. "Them, him or her? Maybe I know your friend, Tara."

"Oh, I shouldn't think so—"

"Why not? If you met him or her – or them – on a field trip, presumably he or she is a geologist. So it's likely that I'd know them – or him." He was taunting her deliberately, she thought miserably. He knew perfectly well she was lying. He had her on a hook and he wasn't going to let her off. "Iceland is a very small community," he went on. "Anyone in a field like geology is going to know everyone else, if only by repute. And there's another reason why I'd be almost sure to know your friend." He paused, while Tara gazed at him. "I happen to know everyone in Heklavik. I know them all very well." He paused again and his smile grew, but she no longer thought it attractive. It was cruel, hard, enjoying her discomfiture. In that moment, she hated him.

"You see," he said softly, and moved his finger to that little red circle on the map, "I grew up in Heklavik. It's where I was born. My parents live there still. So, you see, if I don't know your friend – or friends – it will be very strange indeed."

There was a long silence. Tara looked away at last. She stared at the map and felt the heat of tears in her eyes. How had she got herself into this mess? What on earth was she going to say? That she'd made a mistake, meant to ring some other village where she really did have friends? Jon wasn't going to believe that, not for a moment.

"Why not tell me the truth, Tara?" he said at last, his voice quite gentle. "Are you really planning to try to turn little Heklavik into some kind of holiday development? You must know it wouldn't be at all easy, if not downright impossible. We do have laws, you know. I don't think you'd even get it off the ground."

"I've told you," Tara said, "we don't have any plans at all of that kind." She faced him. "Look, my interest in Heklavik has got nothing to do with the holiday agency. It's – it's something else entirely." She wished again that she could tell him the truth. "It's a personal thing," she said, hoping that he'd let it go at that.

But Jon Magnusson wasn't the kind of man to let anything go. Like a terrier, she thought, he would worry it to death until he knew. If he didn't worry *her* to death first . . . And she wasn't at all sure she could stand up to his questioning. He had the sort of insistent authority that was very hard to defy.

"Can we just look at my itinerary?" she asked, without much hope, but to her surprise, after a long, hard look, he nodded.

"All right. We'll leave it at that – for the moment. But I warn you, Tara, I'm not at all satisfied with this. You're hiding something from me, something to do with Heklavik. And I don't like secrecy, especially when it concerns foreigners coming into my country." He leaned across the table towards her. "You may not be able to tell I'm an Icelander from my voice," he said. "I know my English as is good as any Englishman's, and a good deal better than some. But remember, I *am* an Icelander, through and through. I love my country and I won't see it exploited, not by anyone. So whatever it is you've got in mind for Heklavik, I advise you to drop it. Like a hot potato."

"I told you, I've got no plans for Heklavik—"

"And I've told you I don't believe you. You've lied to me over this, Tara, so why should I take anything else you say on trust?" His eyes seared her face. "It's a pity. I was beginning to trust you, beginning even to have some respect for you. Now that's all gone and I'll be watching you very carefully from now on. Very carefully indeed. Do you understand?"

Miserably, Tara nodded. She knew quite well that she'd been put very firmly in the wrong. Any relationship, any rapport, that might have grown up between her and Jon was now out of the question. Now her every move, her every suggestion, would be scrutinised and suspected.

Not for the first time, she wished she'd never agreed to Mike's request. But what else could she have done?

Chapter Three

"So where do we go first?"

They were in the hotel foyer, surrounded by pieces of luggage, most of it Tara's. Jon seemed to have managed to squeeze all his belongings into one backpack. Or perhaps he had more in the car.

And that was another problem. The car. On Alec's instructions, Tara had arranged a hire car. But Jon, seeing what she had ordered, had shaken his head.

"Not nearly man enough," he'd stated. "You need a far bigger vehicle than that for what you plan to do. We'd better use mine."

"But I don't want—" Tara had begun, but Jon had simply screwed up the papers and dropped them in the bin.

"You don't want to be in my car, at my mercy," he drawled, dismissing her indignant denial. "Well, *I* don't want to be in that flimsy day-out-at-the-seaside toy you've settled for, and not just at your mercy, but in danger from swollen rivers, lava roads and the sort of tracks we'll be using to get to all these places. I thought you'd been here before, Tara. You must have some idea of what we'll be facing."

"Of course I have. And the car's perfectly adequate. It's a four-wheel drive, sturdy and economical—"

"*Economical*? Tara, it's our *lives* you're playing with. All right, it's a four-wheel drive – that's no more than a basic essential. But this car isn't meant for the kind of journey you're talking about. It's for the holidaymaker taking a few tentative steps off the main road. If I understand you right, you mean to go right round Iceland, up into the north. This is just the first stepping-off point, isn't it?"

"Yes, but—"

"Well," he went on, disregarding her effort to reply, "apart from the fact that I think it's a bit late in the year for such an ambitious programme, you certainly need something much more rugged. And with room to carry camping equipment as well as—"

"*Camping* equipment? But I'm not planning to—"

"There may be several things you aren't planning to do, Tara," he said, and she found his blue eyes on hers, looking straight into her mind, "but if you're wise you'll be prepared for any possibility."

There was a long silence. Tara felt her heart begin to thump. She wanted to look away, break that unnerving gaze, but she could not. It was as if his eyes were magnets, drawing her to him, and she felt her lips part as her mind began slowly to spin.

"Any possibility at all," he repeated in a murmur, and Tara had found the strength at last to close her eyes and turn away her head.

Remembering this, she had forgotten Jon's question and heard a note of veiled irritation in his voice as he repeated it. She jumped slightly and then replied with equal sharpness. "Where do we go first? I thought we'd talked about that. Thingvallavatn and Thingvellir, of course. It's the logical place to start any tour of South Iceland, geological or otherwise."

He bowed his head slightly. "I'm glad you think so. I was afraid that the spiritual aspect of the country might pass you by. Or do you mean to talk only about the mid-Atlantic fault?"

"I shan't be talking at all," she said coldly. "I'm just here to work out the possibilities. Alec will be employing guides to accompany the tours."

"And won't you be one of those?" Jon shrugged his pack on to his shoulders and lifted her cases.

"I doubt it. I'll probably have other things to do by then. I don't intend to make a career in the holiday business. And I can carry those, thanks."

"I've got them now." He was striding ahead of her through the big glass doors. Outside, the morning was clear and sunny, with just enough bite in the air to make it exhilaratingly fresh. Tara, still with her own backpack straps only half over her shoulders, found herself scurrying to keep up with him as he marched towards the car park. Annoyed, she slowed down. Why should she always have to run after him, just because he'd been born with long legs?

Ignoring the smaller vehicle delivered by the hire firm earlier in the morning and now waiting to be collected again, Jon stopped beside a large station wagon. He dropped the cases on the ground while he found his keys, then opened the back and swung the luggage inside.

"Good heavens," Tara said, "is this what you usually drive about in? It's practically a mini-bus." She looked inside at the neatly stowed packages, many of which did look like camping gear. "And do you always go prepared for the worst?"

"I'd be a fool not to," he said shortly. "Especially when I'm going into the interior with a foreigner, and a woman at that. He slammed the door and slanted her a wicked look. "Mind you, I always *hope* for the best . . ." He turned away before she had time to take in his words and went to open the passenger door. "Jump in. What are you waiting for?"

What indeed? Tara thought as she moved slowly round the big car. And just what was she jumping into anyway? What had he meant by that cryptic little remark? She climbed up into the high seat and looked out through the big windscreen, wondering just how wise this whole enterprise was. Was she setting herself up for trouble?

The idea of being accompanied on this trip by an Icelander had been no more than an irritation, one she didn't like but had accepted as inevitable. After a year in the Antarctic, living at close quarters with a lot of men – not to mention the many other field trips she had been on – it hadn't even occurred to her to worry about being alone in wild, lonely spots with a strange man. But then she hadn't allowed for that man being Jon Magnusson.

And I should have done, she thought as Jon swung himself up beside her. Mike told me about him. But even he didn't really know what Jon was like, not from a woman's point of view.

She glanced sideways at the man beside her, at the tawny hair, the eyes that reflected the cold, clear light of the Iceland sky. So what *was* he like from a woman's point of view? Had she even got her own thoughts and feelings sorted out?

Handsome, yes, in a craggy way. Lean, yet muscular, positive in his movements, crisp in his speech. Attractive – she couldn't deny that. And yet . . .

Could a man be *too* attractive? Too handsome, too virile, too overpoweringly *male*?

Jon turned suddenly and caught her gaze, and she looked away at once, feeling her cheeks colour.

"Well?" he said. "Ready?" And he let his eyes rest on her face, as if he were asking more than just a simple question.

Ready to go with you out into the wilds of Iceland in your vehicle? Tara thought with a sudden tremor. No, I'm not. I'm not at all ready for this. And she opened her mouth to say so.

But the words died on her lips. How could she say such a thing? How could she admit to fears she couldn't even explain to herself? How could she give up on this before she'd even begun, letting down not only herself but Alec too?

She reached into her mind and found a smile, pinning it on her face like a flag of defiance.

"Yes," she said with all the cheerful brightness she could muster, "of course I'm ready. Let's go!"

The journey to Thingvallavatn was an easy one on good roads, and they were there before lunchtime. As they drove along, Tara forgot her uneasiness. She sat gazing entranced out of the window, almost unable to believe that she was actually in Iceland once again. It had always been one of her favourite countries, so mystical, so fascinating, and like many Scots she felt a strange bond linking her to both the country and its people. Well, some of its people, she amended with a quick glance at the man beside her. But the effect of the wild, empty landscape was too powerful to be spoiled and she turned her eyes away again, watching the scenery unfold before her, her imagination caught as it always was by the thought of its origins.

Out here, away from Reykjavik, there were few buildings, just the odd farm sited where no volcanic danger was expected, or a hut to store animal feeds. On either side empty countryside stretched away towards the distant shapes of volcanoes.

The road they were travelling on now had been driven through the lava itself, its roughness hidden by a covering of soft green moss. A little further on the lava became more rugged, with great plates of rock torn apart by the eruptions. Hummocks that looked like the barrows of ancient burial places stood beside the road, their tops burst asunder by the force of the molten rock that had once come bubbling up inside them, and Tara began to imagine the scene as it must have been in those far-off days.

"We'll park here," Jon said suddenly and she realised that

they had arrived at the waterfall of Oxararfoss. "Presumably you'll want to tell your tourists about the continental drift and there isn't anywhere much better than here to explain it."

Tara nodded and climbed out. From the car park a track led towards the waterfall, and then into the great fissure of Almannagja. She stopped and looked down the line, over a mile long, of fissures that ran parallel with each other like tears in a plank of wood that had been wrenched apart.

"And that's just what's happened here," she said aloud as Jon came to stand beside her. "Only instead of a plank of wood, it's two great masses of land – continents. It's as if on this side of the *gja* we're standing in America, and on that side, in Europe."

Her voice shook slightly as she felt the warmth of Jon's body close to hers. Did he *have* to stand quite so near? He was almost touching her and her nerve-ends prickled like tiny hairs being brushed by an alien hand . . . She shivered and turned quickly away to look at the waterfall, noting the rock structure that would provide another point of interest for her clients. That was what made this country so perfect for the kind of holiday Alec wanted to promote: wherever you looked, there was something fascinating to be seen. Under your feet, above your head, even in the sky, she thought, wondering if there would be a display of the Northern Lights that night. If the sky remained as clear as it was now, there should be a good chance.

But she was finding it unexpectedly difficult to concentrate on the things that might interest Alec's holidaymakers. Jon's presence beside her was becoming more disturbing as for the next hour or so they explored the area, walking along the path which ran along the line of the fissures until they reached the bridge that crossed the river. They paused for a while, leaning over and watching the swirling water. Jon's elbow was close to her arm and she moved away slightly, her body touched by a heat she didn't understand.

"I shouldn't like to fall into that," she commented in an attempt to divert his attention from her withdrawal. "It looks icy cold, not that you'd have time to notice that before you were battered to pieces on the rocks."

"As well you didn't live here in the Middle Ages, then," Jon said lightly. "This is where they used to drown adulteresses and witches. Not that I'm accusing you of being either of those things," he added hastily as she straightened up, her lips already parting in indignation. "I'm sure they threw other criminals over too. I mean—" His lips twitched and he broke into laughter. "I don't seem to be making it much better, do I?"

"Not a lot," Tara said, amused herself. "I suppose that's what you'd call instant justice: just add water and stir. Did they lay it on as part of the entertainment after the laws had been spoken?" The laughter was a welcome relief from tension and she turned, smiling, and then screamed as she felt her feet slip on the wet surface of the bridge.

For a brief, sickening moment, she thought she was about to fall into the seething waters below, to share the fate of those ancient murderers and adulteresses. The roar of it sounded in her ears, she could feel the cold spray on her face . . . and then Jon's arms were around her, holding her strongly, drawing her upright against his powerful body.

Tara leant against him, trembling. Her heart was beating wildly, her skin prickling with shock. She could still hear the thunder of the water beneath them and she shuddered at the thought of what had so nearly happened.

"It's all right," Jon said, his voice oddly gentle in her ear. "It's all right, Tara. You're quite safe. I've got you."

Tara caught her breath, conscious suddenly that his arms were around her, that she was being held close and firm against that warm, strong body. For a moment, she wanted nothing more than to stay there, to feel the length of him against her, to nestle even closer . . . And then her heart, which had begun to slow its rapid thudding, jumped sharply in her breast and her skin tingled afresh, but no longer from shock. Or maybe it was a different kind of shock . . .

She put her hands against his chest and looked up into his face, unaware that her eyes were wide and dark, seeing only the sudden darkness in his as he gazed back. They seemed to reflect the brilliance of the tumbling water beneath and for a breathless moment she stood quite still in his arms, unable either to move or to speak.

"You're quite safe, Tara," Jon said at last, but although his voice was soft there was an odd edge of raggedness to it. "It's a long time since anyone drowned here. You wouldn't really have fallen."

He loosened his hold and Tara stepped away, shaken. No, she wouldn't really have fallen, she thought, raising a still trembling hand to brush a curl back from her forehead. She hadn't been in any real danger. So why had Jon caught and held her like that? And why had she let him?

There was more than one kind of danger here, she thought, glancing again at the uncaring waters. There was too much history, too much atmosphere.

Without looking at Jon again, she moved away. The sooner they were out of this place, the better.

They walked on and found themselves standing on a small stadium, where a flagpole proclaimed that this was the site of the *Logberg*.

"The Law Rock," Jon said, gazing out across the broad, watery plain of Thingvellir. He spoke quietly and Tara listened, knowing that this place, the spiritual centre of Iceland, must mean a great deal to him. "They used to assemble here once a year, all those Icelanders who were able to make the journey, and the Law-speaker would recite the laws from memory. Any new laws would be told, and then the court was held and justice meted out. Instantly, as you said."

He turned and looked down at her and she caught, in the darkness of his eyes, a glimpse of those Icelanders of so long ago: tough, independent men and women who conducted an incessant battle with the rawness of the land which was their home. She remembered her first impression of him – a Viking, ready for battle – and felt an answering movement somewhere in the deepest part of her heart.

Abruptly Jon turned away and walked on towards the lake. Tara followed more slowly, unwilling to break the spell this place seemed to have cast upon them. For a few moments she had felt a closeness with this man that was like nothing else she had ever known. It had crept upon her, wrapping her like a web which she felt enclosed him too, and even though a part of her still cried out in fear, she could not yet struggle free. It was as if he had touched some hidden part of her, some part that had lain sleeping all her life and was now ready to wake . . .

For a few minutes they stood on the top of the cliff without speaking. No one else was in sight. They could have been alone in a world that had scarcely begun. Only the hotel and the few buildings below them betrayed the fact that other human beings existed at all.

"It gets you, doesn't it," Jon said quietly. "The whole atmosphere . . . It does something." He turned and looked down at her and his voice was suddenly rough. "Is this what you'll show your holidaymakers, Tara? Is this where you'll bring them, with their chatter and their inane laughter and their surface curiosity? Because that's all it's going to be, isn't it – the curiosity of people who are just looking for something different, a holiday they can go home and tell the neighbours about? I can see them now with their smart clothes and their cameras, snapping away, making videos to show their friends. 'And this is where they threw the adulteresses,' they'll say, and scream with laughter. And they'll collect a few rocks to display on their mantelpieces, and next year they'll go to Majorca again or perhaps try a skiing holiday and forget all about Iceland. It won't mean anything to them, not really."

Tara stared at him.

"Is that really what you think? That everyone who comes here to see what Iceland is all about comes only to score one over the neighbours? Is that what you think *I'm* like?"

Why had she asked him that last question? What did it matter what he thought she was like? But as she gazed at him, trying to understand what was going on behind those cold blue eyes, she knew that it did matter. It mattered very much.

"Well, what *are* they like?" he asked, and she knew he was evading her real question. "Tara, I've seen them. Coming out of their smart hotel in Reykjavik, getting into a deluxe coach, doing three waterfalls and a glacier in a day and going home with a lot of photographs they can't even identify. No idea of what it is they've been looking at—"

"But our clients *will* know," she interrupted. "I've told you – they'll be people who *are* interested in geology. They'll want to hear about it and explore and find out for themselves, and I believe that having been once, they'll want to come again. And again. As I do." Her voice quivered suddenly and she turned away and stared out over the brooding landscape. "I love this place," she said quietly. "I wouldn't do anything to spoil the atmosphere it has. And in any case—" she lifted her eyes to the majestic slopes of Hekla, one of the most active volcanoes on the island, which had erupted only a few months earlier "—I think Iceland is well able to look after itself. It won't *let* itself be spoiled."

Jon followed her glance and laughed suddenly. "You mean it will show its displeasure with an eruption! Well, maybe it will – who knows?" He turned and began to walk

69

back down to the car park and Tara followed, not quite certain of his mood. Not even, she thought ruefully, quite certain of her own.

What had happened to them here in Thingvellir? Was it just the mystical atmosphere that hung over the silent landscape? A sensation that could be felt by anyone receptive enough, the ghosts of past emotions, past events, that walked here still?

Or was it something more personal – something between herself and Jon? Something that had already existed between them and had been called into life here, where Icelanders had come for a thousand years and more to hear the Law-speaker's words?

Tara shivered. With a determined effort, she turned her mind away and began to look for features that would make the visit even more interesting to Alec's clients.

But, somehow, they didn't seem quite as enthralling as she'd expected . . .

They spent the rest of the morning exploring Thingvellir and although the atmosphere between them was still tense, they managed to maintain a more detached, impersonal attitude towards each other. A colder one too, Tara thought a little sadly, and found herself wondering what Jon would be like with someone he liked – or loved. The thought brought a tingle to her stomach and she turned away from it abruptly. Jon, *love* someone? she asked herself scornfully. Why, he didn't know the meaning of the word!

And she'd be better off to stop thinking about him like that. Think about the place instead, that was what she had come to see, wasn't it? Think about the rocks rather than the atmosphere . . . But that was easier said than done in this strange, evocative place.

"It's easy to understand how so many folk tales have grown up in Iceland," she observed as they made their way to the hotel for lunch. "There's such a strange atmosphere – I feel almost as if we were being watched."

"By supernatural beings?" Jon asked with a half smile. "Trolls, elves, elementals?"

Tara shivered and glanced about her. "Don't! Perhaps it's bad luck to speak of them, let alone joke about them. Do you know many of the stories, Jon?"

"A few," he said off-handedly, but Tara had a suspicion that he regarded them less casually than he pretended. "Most of them seem to be excuses for unwanted pregnancies, dairymaids being 'got with child' by mysterious beings who came in the night, that sort of thing. Country folk were as lusty in Iceland as anywhere else, and as ingenious in thinking up good cover stories!"

Tara smiled, but she still felt uneasy. "I wonder why it is so many old cultures have evolved these stories," she said thoughtfully. "Might there be some truth in them somewhere, a common factor that we ignore today with all our dependence on technology? Why should there be so many stories about elves if they don't exist and never did?"

Jon glanced at her. "Don't speak so loudly, Tara! You may be right in being so sensitive and plenty of Icelanders today are just as superstitious. Even if the elves and trolls don't hear you, a local whose belief is as strong as ever, might."

"Really? I don't think a Briton or an American would admit to being so superstitious these days."

"Maybe not, but they don't live in a land that's still constantly changing. Iceland's shape alters almost as you watch; it's easier to believe in elementals here than in the middle of London or New York, where the only changes are brought about by man – and none of them as cataclysmic as here."

He paused, gazing around him at the deceptively quiet landscape. At the far end of the lake they could see clouds of vapour from the hot springs billowing like the steam from a devil's cauldron.

"There are places here that people still believe to be enchanted," he said quietly. "To the extent that they refuse to allow a road to be built nearby. Look at the map, Tara, and see where the road takes a sudden, unexplained diversion. It might be the risk of subsidence, an underground river or maybe a weakness in the earth's crust, which is so thin here. But it might be something else . . ." His voice dropped almost to a whisper. "No one will risk angering the elementals, Tara. There have been too many stories of people being taken away, disappearing for years in an old tumulus, perhaps, or falling into a sleep so deep no one can wake them, their bodies resting while their souls go journeying who knows where . . . never to be the same again, waking to a world they no longer understand . . ." His voice softened to silence.

Tara turned and looked up at him. He was gazing into the distance, his eyes cool, almost opaque. She had a sudden feeling that he had gone far away from her, that the mysticism of the countryside had invaded his soul, lifting him away and leaving nothing but a shell, as in so many of the old elf-stories.

A cloud passed across the sun. Her skin was suddenly cold, and she shivered. Fear touched her briefly and then was gone as Jon looked down at her with a smile that was wholly earthly, infuriatingly wicked and far too attractive for comfort.

"You almost believed me there, didn't you, Tara!" he exclaimed. "You really thought I'd been abducted by the little people. It's all right, I'm as real as ever, large as life and twice as natural, as you English people say."

"Oh!" For a moment she was speechless. Furious that he'd caught her out and not entirely convinced that he wasn't covering up his own feelings, she glared at him. "I just wish you *had* been taken away!" she exclaimed. "Rest assured, *I* wouldn't have tried to wake you up. And I'm not English, I'm a Scot."

Jon roared with laughter. "And I'm half a one, so between us we rather outnumber the Icelanders present, don't we? But aren't Scots superstitious too?"

"Ask your mother," Tara retorted, walking on quickly. "And while you're about it, ask her to teach you some manners. Though I can't believe she hasn't tried hard enough, poor woman."

Jon's long stride brought him alongside her. "What have you to complain about, Tara? Are my manners so bad? Didn't I carry your suitcases for you? Haven't I driven you here nicely?"

"Driven me crazy, more like," she muttered, and then sighed. "Yes, of course your manners have been perfectly all right. Except that ever since I arrived, you've consistently tried to put me down. You've doubted my professional qualifications, questioned my motives, accused me of wanting to turn Iceland into a chillier version of the Costa Brava and now—"

"And don't you?" he broke in, all trace of amusement gone from his voice. "Don't you want to make Iceland a holiday paradise? You still haven't explained your interest in Heklavik, Tara."

Tara opened her mouth, then closed it again. She'd completely forgotten their argument over that – in fact, for a few hours she'd forgotten all about the mission she'd promised to carry out for Mike Redland. Come to that, she'd forgotten about Mike himself.

And that was quite a step forward, she thought in surprise. But there was no time to investigate that further now. Jon was challenging her with his eyes and she was learning that a challenge from Jon wasn't one that could be ignored.

"I've given you all the explanation you're going to get,"

she said steadily. "There's nothing sinister in my interest in Heklavik."

"So you admit you do have an interest! And if there's nothing sinister in it, why can't you be open? Why can't you tell me?" He waited but Tara remained stubbornly silent and his face hardened. "Very well, then. I thought we were beginning to strike up some sort of rapport. It seems I was wrong." His eyes raked her face. "Don't complain to me any more about my manners, Tara," he said, and his voice was as cold as wind off snow that had lain for a thousand years. "My good Scots mother did at least teach me that honesty was one of the greatest courtesies – especially when you're a visitor in someone else's home."

He lengthened his stride again, moving easily and rapidly away from her. And Tara, left to follow at his heels yet again, stared at his back with hot tears of humiliation scalding her eyes. How was it that he managed to put her in the wrong so often and so effortlessly? And how was it that she couldn't think of a word in her own defence?

If only she could tell him the truth! But Mike Redland had impressed upon her the importance of keeping her errand to herself. Jon Magnusson would be the last person to believe her, he'd said, he would be more likely to be downright obstructive. And without the vital proof, neither would anyone else believe what he had to say.

Only Tara could obtain that proof. And she knew that Mike was right – Jon wouldn't believe her. Hadn't he already displayed his arrogance, his contempt of her knowledge and abilities?

But how she was going to manage it with Jon sticking close to her side throughout the whole trip, she couldn't begin to imagine. Somehow or other, she was going to have to get away from him.

Somehow, she was going to have to escape.

Chapter Four

Jon had booked them both into the hotel at Thingvellir for that night and Tara decided to spend the afternoon visiting the area around Nesjavellir, where they had seen the vapour clouds billowing from the far end of the lake. One of the fascinations of Iceland was its wealth of hot springs, and here they could be seen in all their weird beauty.

"Watch where you walk," Jon cautioned her as she went eagerly towards the main wellhead up the hill. "The silica crust is very thin and if you go through—"

"I'll be boiled alive. I know – I keep telling you, I've been here before." Tara paused to look down into a pool of cobalt blue water, bubbling and simmering in its deep hole. Little fountains of steaming water shot up into the air from its surface and she kept a respectful distance.

"Well, it's surprising how many people forget the danger." Jon came to stand beside her. "There were half a dozen people killed that way last summer, leaping into pools on hot days to cool off and finding too late what a mistake they'd made. Or maybe they never knew – let's hope so."

Tara shuddered. "What a ghastly thing to happen. But that wasn't in places like this, surely?"

"No," he admitted, "it was in the mountains where the streams run hot. They're so often close to glacier streams, which of course are icy cold." He glanced around the strange landscape and Tara followed his eyes, looking at the muddy clay that surrounded the pools. Everywhere steam rose from

75

the surface, betraying the fragility of the earth's crust at this point. Fall through that, and you were in a bottomless hell of steam and surging water with no hope of rescue. She knew that Jon was right to be cautious.

She felt a sudden qualm. It was easy to imagine terrible deeds happening in a place like this where horror lurked so close. As at Thingvellir, there was nobody about – the tourist season was ended and few Icelanders came here during the week – and she felt glad that she wasn't here with someone she distrusted.

And that thought surprised her. Did she trust Jon Magnusson? She considered the question but knew the answer at once: yes, of course she did, as far as her safety was concerned. Arrogant, self-confident and infuriating he might be, but she knew he would never harm her.

Not physically, anyway . . .

She looked at the bare mud, at the clouds of vapour that rose all about them and drifted around the grotesque shapes of lava. No wonder the Icelanders had told each other such strange tales of elemental beings, of trolls and elves; anything could be lurking here, especially in the half-light of dusk or under the unearthly glow of the Northern Lights. She shivered in spite of the heat and turned away.

"Let's go back. I'm not sure I want to bring people here."

Jon gave her an odd look.

"Getting to you, is it? Maybe you've been enchanted. It certainly has plenty of atmosphere." He glanced at the vapour clouds. "More than most places, I'd say, wouldn't you?"

But Tara wasn't in a mood to be amused. She pushed her hands into her pockets and strode back towards the car, thankful for the duckboards that kept her feet away from the thin crust.

"I think Geysir would be enough to demonstrate hot

springs," she said. "It's a bit more civilised there. There's something very strange about this place."

"It's Iceland," he said succinctly. "But as they say, if you don't like the heat, get out of the kitchen. Or the hot springs, in this case. If you really mean to show them Iceland, Tara, you ought to take them to one of these places as well as to the tourist spots. They'll expect it, won't they?"

"I suppose so." She stopped, gazing down the lake where the pipes and buildings of the hydro-electric power station could be seen through more vapour clouds.

"What a strange country this is," she said half to herself. "All this heat and energy simply pouring out of the earth . . . Yet there's almost nothing else here, no stone except what comes from the lava, no trees, no minerals. It makes you wonder why it was settled in the first place."

"It was land," Jon said, "and land means power. It always has done. The Norsemen came here and saw that no one owned it so they took it for themselves. They sent their people here to farm and fish and make what living they could, just so that nobody else would do the same. Hasn't it always been so?"

Tara nodded. "They came to Britain as well. There are so many words here that I recognise. Old country words like 'fell' for hill and 'foss' for waterfall. Seeing those names here makes a link between us."

Jon glanced down at her, his blue eyes suddenly dark, his face unreadable and Tara looked away quickly. What had he read into that remark, made so unthinkingly? That she felt a link between herself and him? But she hadn't meant that at all.

Or had she? Didn't she, in spite of their differences, in spite of the undercurrents of hostility that ran between them, feel some strange bond forming between them? Hadn't she already admitted to herself that she trusted in his integrity, that she felt safe in his company, even in this weird, almost sinister landscape?

And when they talked to each other as they had today, forgetting the reasons why they'd been thrown together, behaving simply as two human beings with common interests, wasn't it true that they were comfortable together?

Comfortable? Tara almost laughed aloud as the word came into her mind. Comfortable, with Jon Magnusson? Why, there wasn't a moment when she wasn't as aware of him as she'd be aware of a hedgehog inside her clothes. Her skin prickled at his nearness, her blood ran hot and tingling through her veins, her bones were maddeningly weak as she walked beside him. No, of all the words she could apply to her feelings when she was in Jon's company, comfortable was the least appropriate.

Comfortable was how you felt when you were with someone you loved, someone you felt at ease with. Someone who was close to you, who could follow your thoughts, who accepted you for what and who you were.

Jon Magnusson had shown no sign of being any of these things to Tara. Nor did she expect that he ever would.

She didn't even want it.

They ate dinner together almost in silence and then Tara announced that she wanted to go to bed early. Since that afternoon a new gulf had opened between them. It was almost as if, every time they seemed to be drawing closer to each other, one of them would rapidly back away. As if they were both equally afraid of what might happen, the risks they might be taking.

Yet what risks could there possibly be? She was only here for a fortnight at the most – hopefully less, since she also wanted to go to the north of Iceland for a similar reconnoitring trip. And as far as she knew, Jon was only accompanying her on this part of the project; someone else had been allocated to her in the north. So in a few days she would leave him behind and need never see him again.

The thought should have brought her comfort, but instead she felt an odd coldness somewhere in the pit of her stomach. As if she were sorry at the thought of never seeing Jon Magnusson again – but that was impossible.

My trouble, she told herself sternly as she prepared for bed, is that I haven't got over the last man yet. I thought I had. I thought I wasn't really all that upset to come home from the Antarctic and find him on the point of marrying someone else. After all, there hadn't been any actual engagement between us. We hadn't been living together. We hadn't made any promises. Just an 'understanding'.

Or – more accurately – a *mis*understanding.

All the same, it hadn't been that easy to adjust to being on her own again, when she'd expected to slip back into being a couple. And she had seen at once that he was not only totally absorbed by his new love, but also ready to defend himself by blaming Tara for her 'neglect'. Any girl would have felt hurt by that, she thought. But she'd tried hard not to show it, even to herself.

'We had a lot of fun together,' Mike Redland had said to her that first evening after she'd come home from the Antarctic. 'And you know you'll always be very special to me, Tara. But when I met Heather – well, it was like being hit by a thunderbolt. I've never known anything like it.' He looked self-conscious. 'It was the same for her too. It was no good either of us trying to pretend.'

Tara had looked at him, seeing for the first time the weakness of his chin, the selfish set of his mouth.

'It's all right, Mike,' she said coolly. 'I'm not heartbroken. You're right, we were just having fun. There wasn't anything serious in it.'

He'd looked relieved. 'And we'll still be friends?'

'Of course,' Tara answered lightly. 'I hope we'll always be friends.'

She'd left him then, thankful to get away without showing him just how hurt she was. And she'd carried that hurt in her heart, refusing to take it out and examine it, refusing to feel the pain of her rejection. Hoping that it would just go away.

But feelings didn't go away, she discovered now. They stayed there, ready to come out again at the wrong moments, ready – if you let them – to spoil the rest of your life . . .

The thought brought her up short. Let *Mike Redland* spoil her life? Let his rejection follow her like unwanted baggage, affecting her feelings for any other man, destroying her trust, making her hold back when she wanted to let go? Had she really loved him enough to let him do that to her?

But I didn't love him at all, she thought in wonder. It was just that we'd been a part of each other for so long, we'd got *used* to each other. Like an old married couple, but without the bonds of a lifetime to hold us together. There really wasn't anything there – nothing at all.

Shaken by her thoughts, she sat on her bed and folded her arms round her knees. For the first time, she allowed herself to feel the pain of Mike's rejection, the feelings she had buried as soon as they had begun to threaten her. And to her astonishment she found that there was really very little pain after all.

What Mike had said was true: they hadn't ever been truly in love. Just playing at it, tasting the emotions, enjoying the fun, delighting in the romance. And if they had made it permanent, what then? What would have happened when the bloom had faded, the romance died? Would they have found themselves still able to love each other?

No, she thought, we wouldn't have loved each other. We'd have been trapped in a disastrous marriage. Mike would have tried to stop my career. He'd have done anything to keep me from stretching myself, doing the things I wanted to do, from living my own life. Because he would have been threatened by that, and he couldn't stand that kind of threat. He wanted to be seen to be the dominant partner, whereas the truth was he did all the clinging. But he would never admit it.

And the pain she had felt? Just hurt pride, she realised now. She hadn't loved Mike, any more than he had loved her. It had been nothing more than a part of growing up.

All the same, she would learn from it. Never again would a man fool her the way Mike had. Or wouldn't it be more true to say that she would never again fool herself? From now on, she would be much, much more careful . . .

Tara unwrapped her arms and stretched herself. She felt as if she had just crossed some important line. As if she stood on a border, looking back over a part of her life that was finished, done with forever. As if she could now look forward with confidence, ready to go on.

But now, she reminded herself, she needed to get some sleep. She slipped out of her dressing gown and dropped it on the chair beside the bed, then folded back the bedclothes. Just as she was sliding into bed, the telephone rang.

It could be only one person. For a moment she hesitated, half inclined not to answer it. But Jon knew she was in here. If she didn't reply he'd think something was wrong and call the manager to open the door. Sighing, she lifted the receiver.

"Tara? Have you looked out of your window?"

"No, I haven't," she said in irritation. "It's dark and I'm going to bed."

"Not so dark as all that. I know it's not geology, but there's one of the most stunning displays of the Aurora Borealis I've ever seen." She could hear the suppressed excitement in his voice. "Come down and meet me in the foyer; we'll walk up the road away from the lights. It really is worth seeing, Tara."

"But I've just got undressed—"

"Then get dressed again, it won't take you a minute. But you've got to see this, Tara. It really is stupendous – look out and see for yourself." He paused, almost as if expecting her to drop the phone and run to the window. "I'll see you in the foyer in five minutes."

She heard the click as his phone went down. Bother the man! Didn't he realise she was still tired from travelling? But he really had sounded as if this was something special and for an Icelander, as accustomed to seeing the Northern Lights as most people were to seeing the stars, that meant a lot.

Tara went over to her window and peered out. Seen from here, the display didn't look all that impressive, but the light from her own room was spoiling it and she knew that he was right: to see it at its best, they needed to get away from the hotel. But did she really want to get dressed again and go out into the cold night air?

As she stood hesitating, she was startled by a sudden pounding on her door. Half scared, half angry, she went towards it, then stopped.

"Who's there?"

"Who do you think?" Jon's voice sounded irritated. "Look, Tara, are you coming or do I have to come in and fetch you?" She saw the handle turn as he tried it. "For God's sake – are you locked in?"

"Well, of course I am!" Thoroughly exasperated, Tara flung open the door. "I always lock myself in in hotel rooms – don't you? And isn't it my choice whether I come and see the wretched Lights or not? I do still have the right to make choices, I suppose?"

He grunted and came into the room. "I can't see anyone daring to take it away from you. Least of all me! Come on,

Tara, I just want you to see them. It really is something special tonight."

"But I was all ready for bed—" Tara began, and saw the appreciative expression dawn on his face as he noticed for the first time what she was wearing, or not wearing, she thought wryly. Brief pyjama pants and a camisole top with shoestring straps didn't leave much to the imagination.

"All ready for bed?" he drawled, a wicked glint in his eye. "Now there's an invitation few men could resist. Maybe we'll give the Lights a miss after all. Unless you think they would help set the scene, as you might say?"

"As *you* might say," Tara snapped, feeling that she must be blushing from head to toe and, worse, that Jon was getting a good view of almost every part of her blush. "There's going to be no scene to set here, I'm afraid. I go to bed to sleep."

"What a waste," he murmured, and Tara turned away and snatched up her dressing gown. As she wrapped it around herself, Jon settled down in one of the big armchairs and watched, smiling. What had got into him? Tara thought crossly. Did he think she was about to perform a striptease?

"Look, it's late and I'm tired," she said, trying to keep her voice calm. "I daresay the Lights will show again some other night. I'll see them then."

"Absolutely right," he agreed immediately, and she gave him a suspicious glance. "So if you really don't want to . . . We'll just sit here for a while, shall we, and have a nightcap together? Or maybe just talk. Open our hearts to each other. What d'you say?"

"No," she said at once. "For one thing, I don't open my heart that easily, and for another I doubt if you've one to open. And I don't want to sit here and chat or have nightcaps or – or *anything*. I just want to go to bed. And you can take that look off your face!" she flashed with real anger. "You know, it's a good thing for you we're not in Britain – we have laws about sexual harassment there. And forcing your way into a woman's bedroom—"

"Forcing? I didn't force – you opened the door of your own free will." He gave her a charming smile. "And all I wanted was for you to come and look at the Aurora Borealis with me. It was your idea to stay here instead. And a very good idea too, if you ask me." He smiled again, slowly, and she felt something twist inside her.

Maybe it would be a good idea to go out after all! The room seemed suddenly small and claustrophobic and she was uncomfortably aware of the wide bed. And hadn't she just made a decision about being careful where men were concerned?

If there was one man who could make her forget that decision, it was Jon Magnusson. And it wasn't because she loved him, or even that she was attracted by him. It was because he seemed to have an unerring knack of confusing her, so that she never knew just where she was with him, what her feelings were, or how she ought to behave. She didn't even know how she *wanted* to behave, curse him! All she knew was that she wanted him out of her bedroom.

And if going to see the Northern Lights was the only way of getting him out . . .

"All right. I'll come. But I'll have to get dressed first." She gave him a pointed look, and he raised his eyebrows, then came to his feet. Well, at least he had *some* manners, she thought as he went to wait in the corridor. All the same, she scrambled very hastily into her clothes. She didn't quite trust him not to come back in without warning if he thought she was taking too long.

Wrapped in sweater, scarf and anorak, she came out of her room to find him waiting at the end of the corridor, gazing out of the window. He turned as she approached and gave her an approving glance.

"Very nice. That bright red suits you and it'll make you easy to spot if you get lost on the lava fields."

"Which I don't intend to do," she said shortly. "You really do find it difficult to believe that I know how to look after myself in wild terrain, don't you?"

"Maybe I do," he acknowledged as they went down the stairs and out through the foyer. "Perhaps it's because you're so small. You don't look quite old enough to have left your mother."

"Whereas you behave as if you were my father," she retorted. "And a particularly overbearing one at that. Oh . . ."

Her words died away as they came out of the main door and looked up at the sky. And she knew that Jon had been right to insist on her coming out. This really was something quite, quite special.

Tara had seen the Northern Lights a good many times now, and she had also seen their counterpart during the Antarctic expedition. But never had she seen quite such a display as this.

Often they were quite white, beginning with a broad streak of light across the sky, lighting it up like a wartime searchlight. She remembered her first sight of them; the way that first wide streak had been joined by others, the way they had moved slowly across the sky so that the stars behind them faded. The gradual expansion of light until in every direction it hung like draped curtains, shimmering folds that seemed to dance as she watched, their brilliance shifting across the great blue dome above her head. She had been enthralled, standing for an hour or more with barely a movement as she gazed at the display that moved so smoothly, so silently through the heavens.

Since then, she had seen further white displays and a few of colours. But never had she seen anything quite like this.

"Let's go down the road a little way," Jon said. "Get away from the hotel lights."

Together they walked into the darkness of Thingvellir. The road was deserted, the broad expanse of plain and lake silent. Away on the horizon, blotting out the stars, Tara could see the bulk of Hekla. At the far end she caught a glimpse of the steaming wellheads, lit by the glow of the buildings around them. But apart from that the darkness was complete.

Except for the display of lights above them. They stopped, staring upwards, turning slowly around in an attempt to take it all in. And Tara felt more strongly than ever before the magic of natural forces; the sensation that all about them were elements of which man still knew nothing.

The Lights covered the sky from the zenith to the distant horizon. They poured down, streaming from one central point to reach every corner of the firmament, a canopy of brilliant colour. Reds, greens, blues, each with the intensity of a precious jewel, constantly moving and changing. The colours merged, blended, then separated again like a shimmering curtain of shot silk, as they covered the entire sky with ethereal beauty.

"There ought to be music," Tara whispered at last. "They look as if they need music."

"They don't need anything at all," Jon replied quietly. "They *are* music, Tara – the music of the night. The music of the heavens, played out in silent symphony." And she knew that he was right. No music made by man could hope to enhance the enchantment of this sight in the haunting stillness of this place, the spiritual centre of Iceland.

For a long time they stood together, gazing upwards. Tara felt almost as if she could fly, soar upwards to become a part of all that moving colour. She shivered suddenly and felt Jon move closer. He laid his arm about her shoulders and she felt his comforting warmth. A moment later he began to sing softly in a deep baritone and she recognised the song from her own childhood back in Scotland.

"The Northern Lights of Old Aberdeen," she whispered, and heard his acknowledgement in the tone of his voice.

'They call them the Heavenly Dancers, the dancers in the sky . . .'

"They do dance," she murmured, watching the shifting colours. "They really do dance." And then she turned in his arms and lifted her face to his.

The kiss came as the most natural thing in the world. It was part of the magic of the night, of the colour that blazed above them. It was part of the enchantment that had spun its web about them in this ancient place, part of the elemental nature of Iceland and the forces that met here.

Tara felt his lips on hers, firm and sweet. His arms held her close against him and she could feel the lean strength of his body even through the padding of their anoraks. His heart beat strongly against hers, and his breath trembled against her mouth. Her own body answered his tremor as she quivered against him, her lips answering his kiss, responding to the sweetness that he gave to her. Bemused, she felt as if she had begun slowly to spin, that if nothing were done to prevent it, she would spin faster and faster until she did indeed begin to soar, whirling out into space to become one with the lights above. Her heart thumped in sudden fear, but even before she could move he had sensed her withdrawal and drawn her more closely against him. His lips moved over hers with a tenderness that calmed her mind yet set her heart beating more rapidly than ever, while her blood sang with the music of the dancing lights.

Jon's hands moved gently over her, shaping her shoulders, her waist, her hips. She pressed herself against him, feeling her body mould to his. Her arms were wound around his neck, keeping his face close to hers, and when he ended the kiss at last she felt her fingers shaking in his thick blond hair.

"Tara," he breathed against her cheek. "Tara, Tara, what are you doing to me?"

Unable to answer, she shook her head and felt him draw in his breath as her hair brushed his skin. She laid her head against his chest and felt the pounding of his heart matching the pulse of her own blood. What was happening to them? What was happening to her?

"It must be the lights," he muttered. "And this place – it's an enchanted place, it has a magic about it . . . Mortals like us shouldn't venture out here after dark. We're likely to be seduced into the hills, trapped by the elves, kidnapped and never be our own selves again . . ."

Tara raised her head and stared at him. What was he saying? Did he believe those old tales? She glanced up at the light and colour that flooded the sky, at the shadowy bulk of the cliffs and mountains that surrounded them. It was as if they were the only two people on earth, the first two perhaps who had stood here, witnessing the beginning of the world. Adam and Eve, before the Fall. Before the Temptation . . .

Jon had loosened his hold and for a moment she stayed, content to be close to him. But now, as the colour began to fade from the sky, the magic too began to disperse. She felt a panic-stricken dismay at what she had allowed to happen. With a sudden gasp, she tore herself out of his arms.

"Tara! What's the matter? Has something frightened you? There's nothing here—"

"Nothing?" she panted, putting several steps between them. "What about all these elves and trolls you keep talking about?"

Jon laughed. "Tara, that was just talk! You surely don't believe I meant it."

"I'm not sure," she muttered. "You sounded as if you did . . . Anyway, it's not that. I just suddenly realised what – what—"

Midnight Rainbow

"What we were doing?" he supplied helpfully, and came close again. "And very nice it was too. Didn't you think so?"

"No! Yes – *no*. Anyway, it mustn't happen again." She backed away from him, wishing they hadn't gone so far from the hotel. "I can't imagine what got into me. Like you said, it must have been the lights. I forgot for a moment—"

"That we were supposed to be enemies?" He was close again and she realised with panic that he was between her and the way back to the hotel, so that the more she backed away the further she was from safety. Safety? she thought with a twinge of hysteria. Hadn't she told herself earlier that at least she could feel safe with this man? Just now he seemed about as safe as an uncaged lion.

"But do we have to be enemies?" he was saying now as she glanced helplessly up and down the dark, lonely road. "Wouldn't it be better if we could be friends? I have a feeling that we could be, you know, Tara. Maybe more than friends. What do you say? Wouldn't it make this whole trip much more comfortable, more enjoyable?"

Tara caught her breath. She stopped retreating and looked up into his shadowed face, wondering if the faint light showed him the expression on her own.

"Enjoyable? Is that what you're thinking – that we could have a nice little fling together while we're doing this job? Haven't you ever heard of the unwisdom," was there such a word? "of mixing business with pleasure?"

"I'm glad you think it would be a pleasure," he drawled. "But as it happens—"

"Well, you can just think again!" she retorted furiously. "I don't know what sort of woman you think I am, or what your own morals are, but I can tell you that I don't go to bed with any Tom, Dick or Harry who kisses me. Or Jon," she added. "In fact, I don't even go in that much for kissing; as I said, I don't know what came over me. But it won't

89

happen again – I can tell you that for free. I'll make very sure it doesn't."

"That's a pity." There was a new, infuriating note of amusement in his voice now. "Because I really enjoyed it and I had an idea you did too. If not, it took you quite a long time to make up your mind just how much you loathed it."

Tara glared at him, then made up her mind and walked past. The road was hard under her boots and she marched quickly towards the lights of the hotel. But Jon, as usual, had no problem in keeping up with her.

"I meant what I said," he told her quietly. "It would be a lot easier if we were friends. If we could trust each other." He paused. "I'm not really sure why you don't trust me, Tara."

"Aren't you?" She stopped and faced him. "Maybe it's something to do with the fact that you didn't tell me who you were when you met me at the airport. And the fact that *you* don't trust *me*. You made that clear from the moment I arrived—"

"No," he interrupted, and now his voice was hard. "It was you who started out with no trust. And I did tell you my name. It was quite a while before I realised you hadn't heard it and by then I'd got sufficiently irritated with you to let you go on thinking I was someone else. It was quite instructive, actually, to see how you behaved with someone you didn't think at all important." His eyes seared her burning face. "I may not have been impressed by you – though I'd like to discuss that with you sometime – but I had no cause to mistrust you. Until you lied to me over Heklavik."

Tara groaned. "You really don't mean to let up over that, do you? You're going to keep on and on in the hope that eventually I'll get so sick of your nagging that I'll tell you. Not that there's anything to tell," she added swiftly before he could pick her up on the words. "I've told you, there's nothing sinister in my marking Heklavik on the map. Nothing at all."

"But you are interested?" he persisted, and Tara sighed, then stopped and looked him in the eye. They were near the hotel now and she could see other people standing outside, gazing up at the sky. She took a deep breath.

"Yes, I am interested. I'd like to see the place. I'd like to go there sometime and maybe spend a day or two exploring the area. Is there anything so strange about that? It must have some points of interest, after all; it bears the name of Iceland's most famous volcano."

He met her eyes and she put all her concentration into holding his gaze. He *must* believe her. So much depended on it. People's lives depended on it.

At last he nodded.

"All right," he said. "We'll go to Heklavik. And maybe then I'll find out what it is you've got ticking over at the back of your mind." His look was straight and grim now, with no tenderness, not even a hint of compromise. "But remember this, Tara, I shall be at your heels the whole time you're there. I intend to know exactly what you do and where you go in Heklavik. If you won't tell me what you're after, I'll find out for myself."

He turned and strode ahead of her, back through the big doors of the hotel.

Tara followed slowly. She stopped before going in and took one last look at the lights that danced above. But their colours had faded now and they formed a curtain of shimmering white light that was itself slowly growing dim. Soon, the sky would be dark once more.

As dark and as cold as her own heart, she thought, and went into the bright, hard light of the foyer.

91

Chapter Five

Tara slept badly that night and woke with difficulty. Her eyes felt swollen and puffy and were reluctant to open and it was only after she had made herself some coffee and had a long shower that she began to feel at all human.

It was irritating, therefore, to arrive in the dining room for breakfast to find Jon bristling with energy and looking as if he'd been up for hours.

"My goodness," Tara said, covering her eyes, "do you have to wear that bright red tracksuit at this hour?"

Jon's eyes passed rapidly over her face and she felt that he knew exactly how jaded she felt. "I've just been for a run. It's a beautiful morning out there, crisp and frosty. Look."

He indicated the window and Tara looked out. The ground was overlaid with a blanket of sparkling white frost and the hills glittered like ice mountains. At the edge of the valley, the basalt cliffs looked like a huge piece of modern art, each rock almost geometrically formed and outlined with a rime of gleaming white. Ice glinted on the pools and in the corner of the window Tara could see a spider's web, white and delicate as fine lace.

The scene lifted her sluggish mood. Entranced, she stared out and felt that quickening of the heart such beauty always brought her. What an amazing country this was, she thought, taking her place at the table. Rainbows at midnight, a fairy palace in the morning. Water that boiled from the earth, fire that erupted from beneath mountains of ice . . .

The thought brought her back with a jerk to the present and her reason for being here. She glanced quickly, almost guiltily, at Jon and found him watching her, a strange expression on his face.

"Don't stop," he said quietly and she stared at him uncomprehendingly.

"Don't stop what?"

"Looking like that. As if you'd caught a glimpse of heaven."

Tara felt her face colour. She helped herself quickly to a crisp roll from the basket. "Maybe that's what I thought it was, for a moment. But it doesn't last, does it? In an hour or two it'll all be gone and look just the same as usual."

"Which you seemed quite happy with, only yesterday," he remarked, pouring coffee. "Yet now you've seen it looking like a fairyland, you can't be satisfied with it again. Maybe that's one of the spells the elves have cast over you, Tara."

"A rather unkind spell, if it is." She glanced out of the window again. "You're right, I was happy with it yesterday. I thought it was beautiful, and it was. But maybe it's just as much an illusion as this is. Nothing really lasts for ever, after all, does it?"

Jon looked at her, frowning a little. "You seem rather disillusioned this morning, Tara. Almost cynical. What's the matter?"

"Oh, I don't know." And if I did, she thought, I don't think I'd tell you. "It's just that nothing seems quite real. It's as if life is playing tricks, showing me this and that and then snatching it away again. Like the frost out there and the Northern Lights last night. You want to stare at it for ever, to keep it somehow in your mind, and before you've really had time to look properly, it's gone. And even though what's left is still lovely, even that can't last. One day, one way or another, it will change."

He nodded. "People build things. Or a volcano erupts. Or an Ice Age creeps over the land. I know what you mean. And here in Iceland, maybe it's easier to be aware of those changes. The Little Ice Age ended here only a hundred years ago. And volcanic eruptions happen all the time."

"And if you can't rely on the world to stay the same," Tara said sadly, "how can you rely on anything else?"

She stared at her coffee, feeling suddenly near to tears. It seemed as if the struggle was beyond her strength, the struggle to live, to become the person she felt she needed to be. How could you even begin the struggle, when everything around you was liable to change at any moment?

"What is it, Tara?" Jon asked quietly. "What's the matter?"

"Oh, nothing." Tara brushed a hand across her eyes and then gave him a bright smile. "Pass me the butter, would you? And then let's look at my itinerary. It's too early in the morning for philosophy!"

An hour later they were once again stowing their belongings in the car. Nothing had been said about their encounter the previous night under the midnight rainbow of the Aurora Borealis. And Tara was thankful for that; remembering it was bad enough, when the memory brought with it a reminder of the sensations she had experienced as she'd stood in Jon's arms, tasting his kisses, returning them, his body pressed against hers, knowing that her own treacherous senses were on the brink of betraying her. She didn't want Jon reminding her as well, not when he could watch her face in the cold light of day and see and understand every expression that passed across it.

"So it's Geysir and Gullfoss today. Rather a touristy sort of day for your ardent geologists, isn't it?" He took her rucksack and heaved it in beside his own.

"I don't think so, particularly. Both are sites of geological

interest, which illustrate different facets of Iceland's structure. They're places visitors expect to see. And it could be
a welcome easy day if it's fitted in between two long trips
– to Laki and Landmannalaugar, for instance."

"Hm." Jon swung himself up into the driver's seat. "Well,
it's your party. You obviously don't feel you need advice."

"I suppose you think you'd have better ideas?"

"Different ones, probably," he said coolly. "I wouldn't
expect *you* to think they were better."

No, I don't suppose I would, Tara thought. She waited
for a moment, then asked, "What would they be, anyway?
I imagine you've been thinking about it."

"Oh, from time to time," he answered with infuriating
casualness. "When I've had nothing better to do . . . For a
start I'd scrap any idea of going to Heklavik."

Tara sighed. He really was just like a terrier with a rat.
"I've told you, there's nothing sinister in my wanting to
go there. I just want to look at the place. Maybe it would
be a good centre for the trip. There's a hotel there, isn't
there? And a folk museum which is worth visiting. Isn't
that justification enough?"

"It would have been, perhaps," he said, "if you'd mentioned it before. But I've got the feeling you've only just
found out about that museum, maybe from the leaflets we
saw back at the hotel. No, that's not why you want to go,
Tara, and at risk of appearing boring, I'd still like to know
just what your interest is."

"You do appear boring," she said coldly. "And I'm
beginning to wonder if your reluctance to let me go there
isn't more sinister than my own interest. Just why do you
want to keep me away, Jon? What's there you're afraid of
my seeing?"

"For God's sake! There's nothing there, *nothing*! Can't
you get that into your head? It isn't worth your while making
the detour—"

"It's hardly any detour at all," she pointed out, "and as far as there being nothing there is concerned . . . so far, you've agreed it's a pretty little place on a nice bay with a stretch of sandur from Hekla's eruptions, a hotel and a folk museum. That's quite a lot for Iceland. Certainly worth a visit, and maybe a night's stay, wouldn't you say? Anyway, I thought we'd agreed we were going there."

Jon sighed. "All right, we agreed. I was just pointing out that it's going to be a waste of time. And time's precious; the weather this morning shows that the temperatures are dropping pretty fast. We ought to make these long trips you're talking about as soon as we can."

Tara had to admit that he was right. September in Iceland could be quite mild, even warm when the sun shone. But it was just as likely to be cold, icy and bringing the first snow of the winter. She didn't want to have to go back to Alec and tell him she hadn't been able to do the most important trips because she'd left it too late, weatherwise.

"We'll go to Laki tomorrow," she decided. "And Land-mannalaugar the day after. And then Heklavik." She glanced out of the window. "Where are we now?"

"Climbing up road 365. There are some caves over there, only a couple of small ones, but they were inhabited until the nineteen twenties. The rock there is quite soft and the caves were scooped out by hand. They look most uncomfortable."

"Poor souls," Tara said. "But we have a few places in Britain where people lived in caves until quite recent times, and they seem to have survived all right. Some of them didn't even want to move."

She gazed out as Jon manoeuvred the station wagon up the bumpy road, lurching between potholes and rocks, its wheels grabbing at loose gravel. This road was typical of so many in Iceland, once you had left the main ring road that went round the entire island. Hewn out of rock and lava or scouring across loose volcanic ash, it could be changed in a day by wind and weather. A storm could whip up a sandy surface and leave bare rock, heavy rain could wrench stones and boulders from their resting places and send them piling up on steep bends, leaving deep holes in the road above. You could never be sure that the road you had negotiated successfully a few weeks ago would be in the same condition now, and Jon had been right when he had pointed out the dangers of travelling alone or without the proper vehicle.

That was the trouble with Jon, she thought, watching the rugged scenery pass. He nearly always seemed to be right. It would make a welcome change if, just once, he could admit to being wrong.

The distance to Geysir wasn't far but the road conditions made the journey a slow one and there was plenty of time to look at the scenery and think of the struggle the Icelanders had endured to make a life here. She was reminded suddenly of her thoughts at breakfast that morning – the struggle to be the person she needed to be. The person she was, deep inside.

The Icelanders' struggle was like that. Harder, for their lives over the centuries had been lives of constant effort and turmoil, as glaciers swallowed their farmland and volcanoes rained fiery ash upon their heads. Yet the result had been strong, independent people who were not afraid to be themselves. People like Jon.

You can't be yourself without a struggle, she thought. Because if you don't fight, the others will win, the ones who want you to be like them. People who are afraid to let you be yourself and try to control you. People like Mike Redland.

She felt a sudden shock of recognition and realised that she had never faced this fact about Mike before, never realised that during their relationship his one aim had been to control her. To manipulate her into doing what he wanted her to do. To keep her by his side, an extension of himself. Someone he could show off, someone who would boost his own image in his own and other people's eyes . . .

"You're deep in thought," Jon remarked suddenly and she jumped slightly. "I suppose you'll say they're worth more than a penny."

"Oh, much more," Tara said lightly, recovering herself. "We've had a lot of inflation since that price was set. Anyway, I don't sell my thoughts."

He smiled slightly. "Very sensible. I just wondered if during all that deep meditation you'd noticed we're in sight of Geysir."

"So we are!" She leaned forward, thrilled by the sudden view of the spout of water from Strokkur. Still several miles away, it rose into the air like a fountain, holding its height for a minute or more before dying away. A small cloud of vapour hovered over the spot for a few seconds, then evaporated, and the scene was quiet once more.

But not for long. Strokkur erupted once every seven minutes and they had seen the surging fountain several times before they finally arrived at the car park. A small crowd of people stood around the erupting waterspout and Tara jumped out and went forward, going first to pay her respects to Geysir itself, now a pool of quiet blue water within the silica cone that had built up around it during the years of its activity. It had stopped gushing now and Strokkur, a few yards away, had taken over as the main tourist attraction.

"It seems sad, though, doesn't it?" Tara remarked as Jon came to stand beside her. "He's the grandfather of them all, the Geysir all geysers are named after, and now he's just too old and tired to go on."

"Well, he's provided us with a promising apprentice." Jon nodded to where Strokkur was erupting again, sending

Midnight Rainbow

a spout of boiling water sixty feet into the air. "And there are plenty of little ones coming along."

They wandered amongst the pools for some time, looking down at the clear water from which baby fountains spurted as if learning the trade, while in other pools the water was coloured by mud and bubbling like some primeval stew. Steam drifted in clouds across the bare landscape and Tara again had the feeling that she had strayed into another world.

She glanced around. She had wandered away from Jon to a part where few people had come, and stood alone gazing through the steaming air. She had the sensation that she stood on the brink of some significant change in her life, as if she had come here, not only to reconnoitre for Alec's holiday agency, and to carry out Mike's errand, but on some mission that was much more deeply concerned with herself, with her own development, with her whole life.

Tara shook herself impatiently. She really was letting this place get to her! She already knew what she wanted to do with her life. Live it as she was doing now, going to interesting places to explore and find out about the world. The real world of stone and rock, the world that man hadn't made and could never really destroy. Because it could always win. With volcanoes, glaciers, storms and earthquakes, the earth could always win.

And Tara wanted to know about that world. Because the more you knew about it, the more certain you could be that it wouldn't let you down.

She saw Jon walking towards her and turned away abruptly. Couldn't he leave her alone for a minute? Did he too have to have control – was he just another man who couldn't function alone, who needed a mirror?

Well, I'm not going to be that mirror, she thought. I'm too concerned with being myself to want to provide someone else with a reflection they feel comfortable with.

99

"Ready to go now?" she asked brightly as he came level with her. "I think we've seen enough, don't you?"

Jon gave her a quizzical glance. "What's this? Playing the blasé sightseer now, are we? I thought you were bowled over by all these tourist attractions."

"I don't consider Geysir a tourist attraction," she snapped. "I told you before, it's something every visitor wants to see, and rightly so. And I'm not blasé, I just think we ought to get on if we want to see Gullfoss as well."

"Just what I was coming over to say," he replied blandly. "It's a good day for rainbows but we'll miss the best ones if we don't go soon."

And as usual he was right, Tara thought, when they stood an hour or two later gazing at the torrent of water that flowed down the river to hurl itself over the great cliffs and canyons of Gullfoss. The wide curve of the river swept over the great cliff, splintering into a million tiny droplets of white water as it hit the floor of the canyon and thundered away through the deep gorge.

And over it all, like a bridge to heaven, hung the iridescent bow of an enormous rainbow, its colours caught and echoed a hundred times in the spray beneath.

"It's a magic place," Tara said in a low, awed voice, and she turned and looked up at Jon, feeling oddly shaken. "You know, I've never felt it quite so deeply before, the magic of Iceland. It seems stronger than I've ever known it, wherever we go. Thingvellir, the Lights last night and now this. What is it? What's happening?"

His eyes were on hers, wide, intent, the changing colours of the waterfall reflecting in their darkness. She felt breathless as he moved closer and laid his hands against her cheeks. He tilted her face up towards him.

"I don't know," he murmured, "but whatever it is, it's happening to me too. The magic, the power. The elements we know so little of. It means something, Tara, something to you and me." And as she closed her eyes, she felt his lips brush hers very lightly. She felt the sweetness of his breath, the tenderness of his mouth against hers, and without thinking she slipped her arms around him and let her lips part under his.

The roar of the waterfall sounded in her ears. It seemed to tremble through her body, pulsing with a promise of power that could end only in the kind of release that could generate an energy of its own, mighty enough to create its own life, its own continuation . . .

Fear quivered through Tara's body, but Jon gathered her closer, giving her no chance to escape. She knew that the insistent rhythm throbbed as wildly through his body as through hers. She could feel it in his kiss, in the movements of his lips, and she could feel the almost unbearable restraint that he was exercising. As if mesmerised, she let him explore her mouth, his tongue teasing her own, his teeth grazing the soft inner flesh of her lips, and she felt the tension mount in her own body, the tingle in her breasts, the warm ache in her thighs.

Jon touched the corners of her mouth. He kissed her eyelids, her nose, her hair. Then he lifted his head and looked down at her, and she saw the grave look in his eyes.

"Do you know what's happened to us?" he whispered, and even though the roar of the waterfall drowned his words, she knew what he was saying. "Do you know what magic this is?"

"Jon," she said uncertainly, "I—"

"Don't run away from it, Tara. Don't run away from me." His arms were hard about her body. "It's as elemental as the land itself, this magic. And it's something we can't fight, shouldn't even try to fight."

"Jon, I don't want—"

His voice was low, barely more than a whisper. "You don't want to give in to it. You don't have to tell me that,

Tara. I've watched you trying to resist. But it's happening all the same, isn't it? It's too strong, too strong for either of us . . ."

She shook her head. "We don't even like each other—"

"Like each other? What does *liking* have to do with it?" His eyes glittered and he bent his head to touch her lips again. She felt her eyes close and whimpered softly. "You see, Tara," he murmured against her mouth, "when we're like this we're both on fire. You can't deny it."

Tara stood helpless in his arms. Once again she could hear a roar in her ears but could not tell if it was the sound of the great fall or the tumult of her own blood. She felt Jon's lips on her face, her eyes, her neck, and she trembled, yet could not turn away. She felt his fingertips on her breast and knew that her body was straining towards him, even though her mind was telling her to resist.

But that voice in her mind was growing fainter. In a few moments, after a few more kisses, she would be unable to hear it at all . . .

"Please," she whispered with an effort, "please, let's go now."

There was a moment of stillness. Even the mighty waterfall seemed to hold its breath. Then, with a strange mixture of relief and regret, she felt Jon's arms loosen and knew a sudden chill as he shifted his body away from hers.

"You mean that, Tara?"

She hesitated. Did she really want him to let her go? Did she really want to walk alone, without the warmth of his arms about her, the strength of his body against hers?

She had a strange feeling that if she told him to let her go now, he would never touch her again. Never kiss her. That whatever had been happening between them would be stopped for ever, never to be repeated.

Was that really what she wanted?

She looked up and met his eyes. If only she could

102

read his feelings there. If only she could know . . . But Jon's eyes were veiled, as dark and enigmatic as the great mountains that reared behind him. There was no way of telling what thoughts lay behind them, what feelings burned in his heart.

And she remembered her resolution, made in the hotel bedroom. Next time she would be more careful. Next time she would not be so ready to trust . . .

"Do you mean it, Tara?" he repeated, and she caught the edge in his voice. An edge of urgency, impatience.

Impatience! It was enough to make her step back out of the circle of his arms and fling him a haughty look.

"Yes, I do mean it," she said quickly, before she could think again. "I didn't come here for a light romance. I've got a job to do and I'd like to get on with it, if you don't mind."

Jon stared at her, but his eyes were no longer unreadable: the anger in them was all too plain. Tara bit her lip, regretting her brusqueness, but knew that it was too late now. The warmth, the fire, had died down as quickly as it had flared up. And in the midst of her regret she knew that it was better so. Whatever it was Jon had had in mind when he kissed her, it could have done no good. It could only have stirred up emotions that were better left alone, bringing pain and unhappiness in their wake.

I don't want to be involved with Jon Magnusson, she thought as she followed him slowly back to the station wagon. The risks are too great. We're better as enemies than as lovers.

And she shivered, wondering why she felt so cold.

Back at the hotel she went to her room and ran a hot bath. She lay watching the scented steam rise about her and thinking over the events of the past few days. It seemed years since she had left Glasgow Airport, years since her first sight

103

of Jon at Reykjavik. She felt as if she had known him all her life. As if she had been only waiting for the moment when they met, as if the previous twenty-six years had been nothing more than a preparation.

That's ridiculous, she told herself sharply. I don't believe in all that 'one man for one woman' stuff. And I don't believe in destiny. It's this place, all this talk of magic and enchantment and elemental beings. It's getting into my brain.

Impatient with herself, she stood up abruptly, letting the hot water cascade down her body. The bathroom wall was lined with mirrors, clouded with steam and she could see herself, like a nymph glimpsed through morning mists, her naked body shimmering as if swathed in silvery gauze. She stood quite still, gazing at herself as if she were looking at a stranger, letting her eyes move slowly over the half-obscured lines of her own body.

Not long ago, Jon Magnusson had held that body in his arms. Only a few short hours ago he had stroked and caressed her, laid his lips upon hers, let them move gently, yet with undoubted passion, over her face, down her neck, into the cleft between her breasts. Not long ago, the body that shimmered in the clouded mirror had been aroused by his touch to a strength of desire that Tara had never experienced before in her whole life. It had needed only one more kiss, one more tiny caress, and she would have been unable to resist him any further. She would have been his, there beside the waterfall with the roar of the cascade in her ears and the rainbow glowing all about them.

But fear had stopped her. The fear of committing herself again to a man. The fear that – she recognised with a shock – had driven her away to Antarctica, away from Mike, and had brought her now to Iceland.

The thought had no sooner entered her head than Tara pushed it away. She reached for a towel and wrapped it about her body, hiding it from her own view. Turning her back on the mirror, she began to dry herself with brisk strokes, rubbing until her skin glowed. Then she sprayed herself with a light perfume and walked back into the bedroom to dress.

It was a pity, she thought, surveying her wardrobe grimly, that she had brought only two garments suitable for the hotel restaurant. She would far rather have gone down to dinner wearing jeans and a sweater than the silky little number in pale silver that draped itself about her body, or the soft blue with the cowl neck that framed her face so well. The thought that Jon Magnusson might get the idea that she was setting out to be alluring didn't appeal at all.

But there was no help for it, and she decided on the blue as being the less provocative. Determined not to give him cause to think that she had changed her mind, she flicked no more than a gloss of colour on her lips and brushed her hair, then pinned a bright, impersonal smile on her face and left the room.

Jon was waiting in the lounge. She saw his blue glance move over her and caught the gleam of appreciation that lit his eyes. He stood up and indicated that she should sit down.

"A drink? I ordered gin and tonic, but it can be changed if you'd rather have something else."

"I would." There was no way she was going to let him decide what she'd drink! And it might be better to steer off alcohol altogether. "I'll have a tomato juice, please."

He nodded and signalled to the waiter. A few moments later, a large glass of tomato juice was placed before her, together with the menu.

"What would you like to eat?" he inquired. "By the way, I'd like to pay for dinner tonight. I know your employer's footing the bill overall, but I also know that that means you try to keep expenses down. And tonight, well, I thought it would be pleasant to have a little celebration. What do you say?"

Tara stared at him. "Celebration? What are we celebrating?"

Jon lifted his glass and leaned towards her a little. His dark blue eyes were smiling.

"A fresh start," he said softly. "A new understanding. Doesn't that seem a good idea?" He studied her face for a moment. "This afternoon you said we didn't even like each other. But how can we either like or dislike when we don't even *know* each other? Tara, I think we've got off on the wrong foot. I think if we started again, gave each other a chance, met each other halfway without any preconceived notions about each other, we could find quite a lot to like in each other. And wouldn't that be a good thing?" He touched his glass lightly against hers. "Friendship, Tara," he murmured. "That's all I'm talking about."

Tara hesitated. It was very difficult not to respond to the warmth in his eyes and his voice, the words he uttered so reasonably. And it would be much nicer to be friends than enemies, she admitted. It wasn't in her nature to be so prickly, so hostile, and she didn't really know why she was. Always before, she'd met new people with a smile and an outstretched hand, always made friends easily. But somehow, in the past few months, she had felt as if she had brought back some of the ice of Antarctica in her soul. Somehow, everything seemed to have changed.

Everything – or just herself?

Perhaps I should do as he says, she thought. Meet him halfway. Make a friend of him, as he says, and make sure it goes no further than that.

"Tara?" he prompted, and tilted his head to one side. He looked exactly like a puppy she had once had, who used to do that whenever he was puzzled or wanted a stroke.

Tara smiled suddenly. She lifted her own glass and touched it against his in response.

"All right," she said. "I'll drink to that. Friendship." And no more than that, she added silently. Absolutely no more than that.

The Antarctic ice had not completely melted. There were still some splinters there, lancing her heart.

They went in to dinner soon after that. The menu was more extensive than Tara had expected, but although Jon insisted that this was his treat and there was no need for economy, her choice was still modest. Friends they might be, but she still wasn't sure of his motives and had no intention of being beholden to him in any way.

"No," she said, "I won't have puffin. I know they're part of the staple diet of Iceland and it's pure sentimentality on my part and no different from eating chicken or duck, but I just couldn't eat one. I'll have a prawn cocktail."

"*Prawn cocktail!*" he exclaimed. "How suburban and Sixties can you get? Just how long were you in the Antarctic, Tara?"

"A year. Not long enough to forget how to be civilised. And I don't eat horses, either." She gave him a defiant glance and he grinned and put up both hands.

"All right, all right, I give in. We're a rough, primitive lot here in Iceland. And so would you be, if you'd been brought up in such a harsh country. People have to eat whatever's available, Tara, and it's not always possible to be so choosy."

"I know. I don't deny it's been necessary in the past. But now – eating puffins, catching whales – is it so essential now?" She glanced at the menu again. "You've got resources other countries don't have, heat and energy boiling up out of the ground, costing hardly anything to produce. You're even growing your own bananas! You could do almost anything."

"And despoil the land to do so?" he asked quietly. "What you're suggesting is a land under glass, Tara. You know perfectly well we don't have either the climate or the soil to grow crops. Do you want us to turn Iceland into a vast greenhouse, just to use up all that free heat you talk about so glibly?"

Tara hesitated. She knew that nothing was ever that simple. The Icelanders would argue as passionately for their right, their *need*, to fish and to catch whales, to make use of whatever harvest Nature provided, as a farmer in Britain would argue for his right to grow wheat. Each changed the landscape, each meant that some kind of wildlife would suffer. Man could not, it seemed, exist at all without causing damage to other creatures.

Most telling of all, she had seen this in Antarctica itself, where man had hardly begun to tread. Yet the marks of his actions had shown themselves in the penguins who bore traces of insecticides in their bodies, in the debris and pollution that had drifted into its oceans, into the ozone layer that hung tattered and torn immediately above.

"I don't know," she said at last. "I don't know what the answer is. Moderation, I suppose. Not taking more than we need. And trying to put something back."

"Yes," Jon said thoughtfully, staring into his glass. "I think you're right. That's just about all we can do. And as a recipe for life, it doesn't sound too bad to me. Not taking more than we need and trying to put something back." His eyes lifted suddenly and stared straight into hers. "Is that how you try to live, Tara? Is that the principle that guides your life?"

Tara caught her breath. His blue glance riveted hers and she could not look away. It was like staring into the depths of the ice, as she had done so many times in

Antarctica, trying to understand what was concealed in that unfathomable deepness. A whole unexplored world had lain at her feet, an abyss of valleys, mountains, lakes and rivers, all overlaid by an impenetrable density of ice. And she had the same feeling now that behind Jon's gaze there was an unexplored world, a depth of understanding that, if only she could plumb it, would lead her to the world where she longed to be. "Tara?" he prompted softly, but before she could find a reply the waiter was at her elbow with her first course.

The moment was gone. And after that, as if both were afraid to explore further, they talked of other things. The sort of things people would discuss on a first date, she thought wryly. Books they'd read, shows they'd seen, music they enjoyed. Holidays, people, news, the stuff of small talk, of getting to know another person. Of making friends.

Somewhat to her surprise, it seemed that they did have many interests in common. Both liked thrillers and crime, especially suspense, as well as more thought-provoking novels. Both enjoyed and had seen every one of Kenneth Branagh and Emma Thompson's films, especially the Shakespearian ones. Both liked classical music, although Tara preferred Tchaikovsky as against Jon's Wagner. And both confessed to a liking for the Beatles, especially Paul McCartney.

"I like a lot of modern music too," Tara said, "but Alice in Chains leaves me cold."

"Alice in *what?*" Jon asked, and she laughed and took him through a resumé of the modern pop scene that left him baffled.

"Don't you have this sort of music in Iceland?" she asked.

"I'm sure we do. But not where I go. I told you, the Beatles are as up to date as I want to go."

They both laughed and Tara sat back in her chair, feeling more relaxed than she had done since arriving in Iceland. No, even longer than that. Since arriving back from Antarctica and being met with Mike's bombshell. At the memory of that, her smile faded and Jon leant forward at once.

"What is it, Tara? A moment ago you were happy, now you're looking sad again. What is it that's making you unhappy?"

She stared at him. "What do you mean, sad *again?* What makes you think I'm unhappy?"

"I can see it," he said quietly. "I can see it in your eyes, I can hear it in your voice. I can tell it from the way you react, as if something has hurt you badly and you want to lash out but are afraid to do so. Or maybe because you're too nice to do so."

Tara looked down at her plate, her eyes stung with sudden tears. How was it that this man, whom she hardly knew, could touch her so deeply?

I can't let him, she thought. I can't let him get close.

She looked up, forcing herself to meet his eyes, and smiled brightly. "You're going too deep for me. I haven't been hurt and I don't want to lash out at anyone. I'm here to do a job and, if you must know, I'm feeling rather guilty about living it up in this very nice hotel and enjoying smart dinners all at Alec's expense—"

"I've told you," he cut in, "tonight is at *my* expense—"

"No. I'd rather not, thank you. I haven't chosen anything I would be ashamed to put on Alec's bill, so I think we'll leave things as they were." She glanced at her watch. "And now I think I'd better be going to bed. We've got a long day tomorrow—"

"Which we haven't even begun to discuss," he broke in again smoothly. "And if we want to make an early start, we ought to do that first, don't you think? Don't you agree we should discuss it?"

"Well – yes," Tara stammered, caught unawares. "But all my papers and maps and things are up in my room—"

"So let's go there, shall we?" He glanced around the crowded room. "You must admit it's not easy here." He rose to his feet and held out his hand. "Come along, Tara. Remember our pact? Remember our toast to friendship?" He smiled. "Why not just relax again, as you were just now, and enjoy it. It's all here for you to enjoy, so why not take whatever Iceland offers?"

Bemused, hardly aware of what she was doing, Tara put her hand in his and let him lead her out of the restaurant.

Her heart beating fast, she unlocked her door. She wasn't at all sure this was a good idea. And when Jon followed her into the room, she knew for certain that it wasn't.

"Look," she said, facing him, "don't you think it would be better if we just went to bed?" She saw his eyebrows lift and her face flamed. "I mean, if we just said goodnight and left it at that? There isn't anything to talk about, is there? We just got a bit carried away. It didn't mean anything, not really."

"Is that really what you believe?" he asked. He was standing close and she felt the warmth of his body. She moved away, wishing she could trust her own senses to behave. How could she talk rationally and calmly when her blood was thundering round her body, her legs were weak and her breath came ragged?

"Well, I have to, don't I!" she exclaimed. "I mean, we hardly know each other, we only met a few days ago and we've done nothing but fight—"

"Oh, that's not true," he interrupted. "We've definitely done other things than fight."

Tara felt her face burn again. "Well, that's just it. It's either one thing or the other. It's crazy. I don't know—"

"You don't know what's happening to you?" He moved towards her again and took her in his arms. "Hasn't anything like this happened to you before, Tara?" he whispered. "Haven't you ever desired a man?"

111

She shook her head. "I don't know. I've never felt like this before. As if I've lost all strength, all power." She looked up at him. "Jon, I don't like it – it scares me."

"But why? You should be happy, excited."

"Because I don't want to be taken over!" The words burst out of her. "Because I want to be my own person, *myself*. I don't want someone else taking over my thoughts, my mind. It frightens me."

He stared at her. "But why should I want to do that? I have my own thoughts, my own mind. If I want you, Tara, it's *you* I want, not some idea I have of how I'd like you to be. You, yourself. Can't you believe that?"

"I don't know," she said. "I just – don't know."

Jon bent his head and touched her lips, and she felt the now familiar sensation of being swept away, carried into a land that was sweet and unfamiliar. She quivered with a mixture of excitement, desire and fear, and he stroked her hair with one hand, soothing her.

"You're shivering, Tara. What is it? What's frightened you so much? You don't have to be frightened of me. You can trust me. Try, Tara. Let go of your fears and trust me . . ."

He laid his mouth on hers and she sighed and slowly relaxed against him. She wanted to trust him, she wanted it badly. But . . .

The telephone buzzed and Jon took his lips away and looked quizzically down at her.

"Shall we answer it?"

"I suppose we have to." She watched as he moved across the room, then felt a sudden twinge of fear. "No!"

Jon stopped and looked at her, surprised.

"What's the matter?" he asked. "It'll only be reception, wanting to know if you'd like breakfast in your room."

"Don't answer it," she said urgently. "I've got a feeling – Jon, don't answer it . . ."

112

The telephone buzzed again and he smiled and lifted the receiver. Tara sat down, a feeling of doom like a weight in her heart. And as she watched, she saw Jon's face change and darken. He glanced across at her, and his expression was hard and cold as she had never seen it before. He held out the receiver.

"It's for you," he said harshly. "It's Mike Redland. He wants to know if you've been to Heklavik yet."

Chapter Six

Tara stared at him. Then slowly she took the receiver and put it to her ear.

"Tara?" Mike's voice said. "Tara, is that you? Who the hell have you got with you?"

She closed her eyes. "Who do you think? Jon Magnusson, of course."

She could almost hear Mike strike his own forehead. "*Magnusson*? Oh, my God! That's *all* I need. You've really messed things up this time, Tara."

The injustice of this rendered her almost speechless and she could only squeak her indignation.

"*I've* messed things up? How do you make that out?"

"Well, I thought it was you and started to talk straightaway. So now he knows about Heklavik – which was exactly what I didn't want him to know, if you remember—"

"I remember." She thought of the times she had already earned Jon's distrust by refusing to say why she was interested in Heklavik. "But I don't see how you can blame me for that. Didn't it occur to you to see who was listening before you started blurting it all out?"

"Look, I didn't think that was necessary. I was through to your room; who else would answer the phone but you?" His voice was suspicious. "I never expected to find you entertaining Magnusson, of all people, at this hour of the night."

"Oh, for goodness' sake, Mike! It's barely nine thirty. And I don't know what you mean by 'entertaining'—"

"Nor do I. I'd have staked my life on it that he wasn't your type. But maybe I was wrong, Tara, just as I was wrong about you before. Maybe these cold climates make you susceptible—"

"And maybe you're letting your imagination run away with you again," Tara retorted. "Just remember, Mike, I wasn't the one who couldn't wait . . ." She glanced across the room and caught Jon's eye. He was standing quite still, his hands thrust into his pockets, regarding her grimly, and her heart sank. Suddenly she didn't want to go on with this conversation. "Look, Mike, could you get to the point please? I presume you had some reason for ringing me here. How did you find out where I was, anyway?"

"Obvious. I rang your friend Alec and got your itinerary from him. Pity you didn't think to give it to me too. Anyway, I just wanted to know how things were going, if you'd managed to get to Heklavik yet. But of course, you won't be able to tell me now, will you? Not with friend Magnusson breathing down your neck."

Tara bit her lip in annoyance and wished, not for the first time, that she'd never got herself embroiled in Mike's scheme. It would have been better if he could have come to Iceland himself. But she'd understood exactly why he hadn't been able to and why he'd asked her. And it would have been easy enough if it hadn't been for Jon.

"As it happens, there's nothing to tell," she said shortly. "I've only been here a couple of days, Mike. Even Alec hasn't started to check up on me yet – and he's paying me."

There was a brief silence, then Mike said, "I'm surprised you can reduce something like this to terms of money, Tara. Surprised and disappointed. Maybe you'll give me a ring when you do have some news, all right?" And she heard his receiver go down.

Tara stood quite still for a moment, breathing hard. If I had

Mike here, she thought, I'd take great delight in throttling him . . . And if the issue were just one of money, I'd have equal pleasure in telling him he could keep it. Find someone else to do his dirty work for him. But that was the trouble, wasn't it? There was no money involved and the work wasn't dirty. And she had no option but to go on with it.

Jon moved and she glanced up at him quickly, wondering what he'd made of the conversation. He still looked as grim, she realised, and what was more, he didn't look inclined to be tactful over it. He came towards her and she felt a quick thrill of fear. After all, she hardly knew him. She didn't know how he would react in anger.

"So what was all that about?" he demanded. "A lovers' tiff, perhaps? Or something more?" He was close now, closer than she liked, and when he reached out for her she shrank away. He laid his hands on her shoulders and she felt his fingers strong and firm on her flesh. "Just exactly what's going on, Tara? What's Mike Redland to you? Why should he be ringing you here? *And what's his interest in Heklavik?*"

Tara tried to twist away but his fingers tightened. She looked up into his face. What had happened to the tenderness she had seen in his eyes only minutes ago?

"Mike's nothing to me," she said. "I never expected him to ring me—"

"Nothing?" he broke in. "You expect me to believe that, Tara, when it's obvious the two of you are hand in glove over your interest in Heklavik? Oh, I believe that you didn't want him to ring you – you didn't want me to find out. You didn't even want me to know that you knew him, did you? Yet you must have known that he and I are old adversaries. So just what's going on? You'd better tell me, Tara, and tell me fast. And make it the truth," he added, staring at her with suspicion.

"Please, Jon, let me go. You're hurting me." He released

her shoulders so suddenly that she almost staggered. She backed away from him and then dropped into one of the armchairs, feeling suddenly exhausted. "Yes, of course I know Mike. Geology's a small world, especially in Scotland. I daresay we've got quite a few mutual acquaintances if we cared to sit down and count them. And that's all he is – an acquaintance."

"Lie number one," he said bluntly. "You're a lot more than acquaintances, Tara. What was it you said? *'I wasn't the one who couldn't wait?'* Couldn't wait for what, Tara? I'd like to hear, it sounds as though there's a great little story there. And that other remark you made about me, *'Couldn't you wait to see who was listening before blurting it all out?'* Blurting out what, Tara?" His eyes were like blue fire, burning into her brain. "I think you owe me quite an explanation."

Tara shook her head. "Jon, I'm tired. Can't this wait till morning?"

"No, it can't, and don't try any of those tricks on me, Tara. You wouldn't have been too tired to make love to me if things had gone the way we thought they were going, would you? You'd have managed to stay awake for that!"

Tara gasped. She felt the colour flood into her face, so hot that she was sure she must be burned. "How dare you—"

"It's true," he stated. "You brought me here because you wanted me to make love to you and I, God help me, wanted it too." His eyes darkened. "In fact, I wouldn't be at all surprised if that's not what you had in mind all along. Especially once I'd found out about Heklavik. You were trying to seduce me, so that I'd forget all about your involvement there, or maybe would stop caring." He glanced at the phone and gave a mirthless laugh. "Maybe I should thank Mike Redland for interrupting us just then! Your nasty little plan just might have worked."

117

Tara groaned and covered her eyes with her hand. "Jon, it wasn't like that—"

"Then tell me how it was," he said inexorably.

There was a brief silence. She sat in the chair, her head in her hands, feeling the tears hot in her eyes. What could she say? How could she convince him without breaking her word to Mike?

"I never made any plan to seduce you," she said wearily. "All that just – happened. I didn't even want it, not at first." She removed her hands from her eyes and looked up him. "Please, Jon, believe me."

He returned her gaze. "I'd like to, Tara. Believe me, I'd like to. But if you're not open with me, if you won't trust me, how can I trust you?"

"I don't know," Tara said miserably and wondered why it was that Mike was so insistent that Jon mustn't know the truth. What was the problem between them anyway? How and where had they met and why were they so antagonistic?

"Tell me about Mike Redland," he said. "Who was it who couldn't wait and what for? What is it he's so interested in about Heklavik?" He stared at her, then said slowly, "I wouldn't have thought he'd be in the holiday business. Perhaps geology doesn't pay well enough for him now. Whatever it is, he's the one you're working for, isn't he? It's nothing to do with Experience Holidays."

"I told you that to begin with," Tara said. "I told you Alec wasn't interested in it."

"No, you just said he didn't want to develop it. You implied that you might be using it as a stopping-off place for you visitors. There's a difference there, Tara." He sighed. "You know, I'm beginning to wonder if you even know the meaning of the word honesty. It certainly seems lacking in your vocabulary. And seeing the friends you seem to have, maybe it's not so surprising."

Tara stood up and faced him. She felt very tired but also very angry. Tilting her head so that she could look into his eyes, she spoke steadily, though she couldn't help a quiver creeping into her voice on some of the words.

"Look," she said, "I realise you think you've got grounds for suspicion. I realise it all looks very odd to you. But I do assure you that there's nothing at all sinister in my reasons for wanting to go to Heklavik, nor in Mike's interest. It's just something he asked me to check out for him, that's all. And it's his business, not mine, which is why I won't discuss it with you. Furthermore, there's nothing at all between Mike and me; we're just friends and colleagues. Though if there were, I don't see that it would be any business of yours." She stopped and took a breath. The last words were the most difficult of all. "And lastly, if you think I've been trying to seduce you, how do you think it looks from my point of view? Maybe *you've* been trying to get *me* into bed just to find out why I want to go to Heklavik. Maybe it's nothing to do with feelings at all." And she turned away, furious with the tears that threatened to overcome her and quite unable to do anything at all to stop them.

Jon said nothing. She knew he was standing there, quite close to her, and she half expected that he would touch her, lay his hand on her shoulder perhaps. If he had she might have turned and flung herself into his arms, breaking down completely, and sobbed out the whole story. Afterwards she wondered if that was what she'd really wanted.

But Jon did not move. He stood quite still, saying nothing. She could not even hear him breathing. And after a long time, she drew a deep breath and lifted her head to look at him.

"Very prettily done," he said coldly. "Very touching. For a moment or two, I almost believed you."

Tara stared at him. She felt a deep shock of humiliation, as if everything had been knocked out of her, swept aside by his contempt. And then the vacuum was filled by a rush of fury such as she had never known before in her entire life. "Get out!" she choked. "Get out of here and leave me alone. You talk about *me* being dishonest! There isn't an honest bone in your body. You wanted to find out what I was doing, so you went the age-old way of doing it, and I almost fell for it. Do you know something? I'm *grateful* to Mike for ringing me. He saved me from what really would have been a fate worse than death!" She let her eyes rake him, as his had raked her, with bitter scorn. "I used to wonder about that phrase. Now I know just what it means."

Jon did not move. "I might as well warn you, Tara, that I mean to find out what it is you're playing at, you and that boyfriend of yours. If you don't tell me tonight, you're doing nothing but postponing the moment. So—"

"Not postponing it. It was never on the agenda, and nor is it ever likely to be. And Mike Redland is *not* my boyfriend. As it happens, he's a married man. And I'm not interested in affairs with married men. Or any man who doesn't have the qualities you so conspicuously lack." She flung him a scathing glance. "And now, will you please go?"

Almost to her surprise, he turned and moved towards the door. She watched, unable to believe that he really was going to go away and leave her alone. At the door, he turned, and she saw that his face was like granite.

"Like I said, Tara, you'll tell me sooner or later. I just think it'd be better for both of us if it were sooner." He paused and his voice and eyes were as stony as his face. "And as it happens, I do know that Mike Redland is married. That's another reason why I'd like to know what's going on between you."

He opened the door and was gone. Tara stood for a moment staring at it, then sank down again into the chair.

The next few days were going to be the most difficult of her life. Jon wouldn't, she knew, give up on this. And now that he knew Mike was involved, he was going to be all the more persistent.

But why were the two men so hostile towards each other? What had happened between them? And why did she have to get caught in the middle of it all?

It was a pity, Tara thought next morning as they set out, that she had decided to make the long trip to Laki today. There was nothing she wanted to do less than sit in the station wagon beside Jon for several hours, negotiating difficult roads and not speaking.

Not that either of them would have been any chattier, whatever the plan had been. From the moment they met after breakfast, Tara having decided to have hers in her room to stave off the moment as long as possible, it had been obvious that neither of them was in any better mood than when they had parted the night before. Jon's face was so grim she wondered if it had set in concrete overnight, while hers felt as if a smile would crack it. Their greetings were brief and curt and with a minimum of discussion they were on their way.

After studying the maps, Tara had decided to combine the trips of Laki and Landmannalaugar, though she would suggest to Alec that they should be done separately, to give time for exploration. All she needed now was an accurate idea of road conditions, journey times and what to see along the way. It would be a long day, but with the weather undecided she felt it best to get it done as soon as possible. Ice or even snow was threatened and either would make the journey impossible.

"We've got several rivers to cross," Jon said when she told him her plan. "We'll have to make an early start or we won't make it before the meltwater starts to come down."

"But that's where the cold weather's on our side," Tara

argued. "If the glaciers aren't melting so fast, the rivers won't be so full. I don't think we need worry too much."

Jon shrugged. "Suit yourself. I only live here, of course." And he swung himself up into the driver's seat and started the engine.

Tara scrambled up beside him, feeling ruffled. It was going to be like this all the time now, she thought. Every little change of plan, every small suggestion, disparaged and made a subject for argument. If anything went wrong, it would inevitably be her fault. And if she did ask his advice, he would probably refuse to give it, saying that she was in charge, it was up to her, he was only there to drive . . . and so on.

I've heard it all before, she thought as they travelled along, from other men whose feelings were ruffled. The best thing is to ignore it.

And so she did, remaining silent as Jon drove the vehicle along rocky roads until at last they were climbing high to look down across the valley towards the mighty volcano of Hekla itself. Tara took a deep breath. Here was the beginning of the vast black desert of ash and twisted, grotesque pillars of lava that were a lasting monument to the great eruption two hundred years ago.

"Awesome, isn't it," Jon said quietly. "And once we've crossed the Fossa, we're not far from the settlement that was destroyed almost nine hundred years ago and almost perfectly preserved by ash. Iceland's Pompeii." He smiled grimly. "That was before they knew enough not to build in the path of a volcano."

"But they can never be sure," Tara said. "Nowhere's really safe, is it? A new volcano can erupt at any time, just where it's least expected."

"Hardly likely, nowadays. A very careful watch is kept on the earth's behaviour. Every tremor is recorded and when there are a lot in any one place—"

"But it can still happen – think of Heimaey. Half a town swallowed overnight, and no warning."

"That was almost twenty years ago. Techniques have improved since then."

"So you're complacent?" she said. "You think you've conquered the volcano, here in Iceland?"

Jon glanced at her as if surprised by the intensity in her voice.

"Nobody will ever conquer the volcano. But we believe we've learned to live with it. Once we know an eruption is on the way, we close the area down. Nobody is allowed to be at risk."

"But what I'm saying," Tara said, trying to keep the impatience out of her voice, "is that you *don't* always get warning. Not the way you do it."

There was a very brief silence. Then Jon said coldly, "I take it you're saying our methods are wrong."

"Not wrong. Incomplete."

"Yes," he said, and there was no mistaking the edge of anger in his voice, "and of course, as I said earlier, we just live here. We wouldn't know."

Tara sighed with exasperation. "Look," she said, "try to forget that you're a man and I'm nothing but a second-class citizen – in other words, a woman. Try to imagine we're both intelligent beings and *think* about what I'm saying." The sarcasm was almost sharp enough to cut her own tongue. "I'm not criticising you or your country," she said carefully. "I'm only saying that you can't predict where a new volcano might occur. Obviously you monitor all the known ones. But they were all new once and we know the process hasn't stopped. You don't even need a mountain, fissure volcanos can go on for miles. So what if a new one were to start somewhere completely unexpected?"

"Speaking as one intelligent being to another" Jon replied with equal sarcasm, "we're trying new methods all the time.

Meanwhile, we live with the risks." He concentrated for a few minutes on fording a river. In spite of the cold, the water was still flowing rapidly from the glacier and it rose unnervingly high on the station wagon as the wheels scrabbled their way across the loose gravel bed. Tara glanced out anxiously, glad that they weren't coming back this way. But there would be other rivers to cross, she thought, before they made it back to good roads and bridges again.

The vehicle climbed out on to the far bank and Tara could almost feel it shaking itself like a dog. Well, no water had come in and the engine was still running sweetly, so all was well. She gave reluctant thanks that Jon had insisted on using his own wagon rather than the car she had hired. Four-wheel or not, it wouldn't have been sturdy enough for this sort of terrain.

"Presumably," Jon said at last, "you think we should be able to predict new eruptions. With crystal balls or something." He smiled maddeningly.

Tara felt her temper quicken. "I'm not saying anything of the kind. I'd suggest using scientific means."

"Which we're already doing. With quite modern equipment, you might be surprised to hear. As soon as there's a tremor anywhere—"

"*Which might be too late.* I'm talking about eruptions like Heimaey, where there *weren't* any tremors." She sighed. "Oh, let's forget it. We're just going round in circles." And she turned her head away and gazed out of the window.

Hekla's devastation lay all around them, a barren moonscape that seemed to stretch on for ever. Nothing could be seen but black ash and the gnarled blocks of lava. And the road had worsened. From gravel, they were now driving slowly over bare rock. Deep holes were followed by jagged outcrops. Now and then they would strike a smooth stretch, where it was almost impossible to see which way the track actually ran.

A little further on, the scenery changed again and Jon stopped the vehicle so that they could get out for a few moments. Tara looked around, awed by the weirdly beautiful panorama that lay before her.

They were now travelling over sand, with dunes piled amongst the craggy lava on either side and rimed with frost. Ice sparkled on the lava, turning the whole scene into a fantasy of strange, glittering shapes. There was no sound, no rush or tinkle of water, no birdsong, no whisper of wind. There was no sign of man, no man-made object other than the wagon, no hint that man had ever come this way. No touch of life at all.

She shivered, aware of a vast isolation and suddenly thankful to have Jon with her. To be alone here, without help or company in the event of a breakdown or accident . . . the idea was a terrifying one. And with it came the thought that one didn't *know* that there was no life here in this stark, barren desert.

Scarcely aware that she spoke, she whispered, "Anything could be lurking amongst that lava, hiding behind those shadowy dunes, anything . . ."

"What's the matter?" Jon asked, his voice tinged with amusement. "Scared of the trolls?"

She turned quickly, flushing as she realised she had spoken her thoughts aloud.

"Well, it is pretty creepy," she said defensively. "All these queer shapes, and the silence. Like something out of a fantasy story. I wouldn't be at all surprised to see some elemental being come stalking out of the rocks. I can see why the ancients told so many stories about them."

"Maybe they told them because they were true," he said quietly, and she gave him another startled glance. Did he really believe it? But in this place you could believe anything, and Icelanders were a superstitious people. He

125

might pretend to dismiss it all but she wasn't at all sure that he really meant it.

They went back to the station wagon and climbed into its warmth. Jon produced a flask and poured coffee for them both and they sat sipping it, still gazing at the icy landscape.

What was he thinking? she wondered. Was he enjoying being here, driving across the bizarre landscape that was a part of his heritage? Was he at peace with himself, drawing some deep pleasure from the silence, the isolation? Or was he resenting every minute, aware of time passing, time that was money in his business life? Perhaps he was angry because the government work he did – work that she sensed he did as a patriotic duty – required him to waste that valuable time acting as chauffeur and bag-carrier to a female holiday agent.

Not that he seemed to see himself as either of those things. From the beginning, he'd placed himself very firmly in charge: stalking off at the airport, returning the car she'd hired, dismissing her plans and introducing ideas of his own . . . It was almost as if this were *his* trip, she thought resentfully. And what did that make her? His assistant?

Jon turned his head and met her eyes and she felt a shock of recognition. She was suddenly very aware of him, of his body, hard as a rock yet hinting at a deep, powerful warmth. Like a volcano, she thought, filled with deep, simmering fire. In fact, his whole personality was strangely like that of the country he lived in. Fire, smouldering beneath a covering of ice. A volcano beneath a glacier.

And when he erupted? She knew just how spectacular an eruption could be below ice. A *jokulhlaup*, sending ice and rocks and fire together into the sky, torrents of ice-water mixed with molten lava into the valleys below, a swirling, impossible mixture of the extremes of heat and cold; a battle of the elements, which no human being could hope to survive . . .

"Jon—" she began impulsively, and then stopped. How could she tell him? How could she hope to convince him? If only it hadn't been Mike Redland, of all people. If only there hadn't been this unbreachable hostility between them.

Chapter Seven

"Were you going to say something?" Jon asked politely.

Tara stared at him. Her thoughts had taken her so far and so quickly that she barely remembered having spoken. She shook her head doubtfully, wondering what she had meant to say, and then remembered.

"I was just thinking," she said hesitantly. "All this grandeur," she waved her hand at the empty landscape, "it has a strange effect. Makes me feel rather insignificant. I just wondered – well, about last night—"

"You wondered what it was we found to quarrel about," he said quietly. "I know what you mean. It has that effect on me too. All this has been here for quite a while and will stay for a lot longer. Long after we've been forgotten."

Tara nodded. Jon had rolled his sleeves back and she could see tiny golden hairs on his forearm. His hair was the colour of ripe corn and his eyes were very dark. She felt a melting deep inside her and was suddenly breathless.

"So," his voice was very soft, "are you suggesting we make love, not war?"

Tara gasped a little. She hadn't intended to put it as bluntly as that – but was that what she meant? She shook her head in hasty denial.

"I only meant that we could be friends," she said quickly, feeling the colour heat her cheeks. "Quarrelling in a place like this, well, it seems so childish."

"Oh, I agree." He gave her a slow smile.

She was even more aware of him now, and equally aware of their isolation in this place. Why on earth had she started this? she wondered. She hardly knew this man, after all, yet here she was, virtually at his mercy in one of the wildest and most remote places on earth. And he must know how magnetically attractive he was. No doubt he expected every woman to fall at his feet, begging for his favours. No doubt he was all too well aware of exactly the effect he was having on her now.

"So that's all right." She kept her voice bright, even managed to inject a little briskness into it. "Shall we go on? We've still got a long journey."

"Indeed we have." There was a smile in his voice, as if he saw some deeper meaning to the words, but he turned away from her and started the engine. "However, before we actually go," he turned back and leaned towards her, and her moment of relief evaporated, "let's seal our bargain in the time-honoured way, shall we? With a kiss?"

A kiss was the thing Tara wanted least, yet desired most. Her heart skipping, she leaned away, but she knew it was no more than a token. There was no escape here. Jon reached out a lazy arm and drew her close and she came unresisting. He touched her lips with his, gently at first, then firmly, and her blood leapt in response. She felt his arms close around her, warm and strong, and she knew there was no way of stopping her own winding themselves about his neck. She felt his smile against her mouth, and as his tongue touched her lips she let them part in invitation. His hand moved to her breast, warm and strong, and then, very gently, he ended the kiss and drew away.

Tara found she was trembling. She laid her head on his shoulder, bewildered. What was it this man could do to her? How could she hate him one moment, love him the next . . . ?

Love him? She caught her breath. What was she thinking?

Love Jon Magnusson? No – impossible. But if it wasn't love, what was it, this leaping of her blood, this kicking of her heart? What was it that drove her into his arms?

Jon put her back into her seat and gave her another slow smile before settling himself ready to drive on.

"Let's talk about it later, shall we?" he said, putting the engine into gear. "As you say, we still have a long journey ahead of us. And I think we have quite a lot to discuss, you and I."

He slanted her another glance, then gave his full attention to the track ahead. Tara sat silent and subdued, wondering just what he'd meant by that remark.

She didn't have the slightest illusion that he'd forgotten about Mike Redland, the telephone call of the night before or her interest in Heklavik. Nor did she think that any discussion between them would omit those points. The reckoning would come, sooner or later, she thought, and began to understand how prisoners under interrogation could eventually tell their captors anything they wanted to know.

But captors didn't usually make love to their victims. Or was that just another form of torture?

By mid-afternoon they had crossed the great rocky expanse of Landmannalaugar and visited the lonely outcrop of Laki. The mountain itself was not especially high; in an hour they had climbed to the top and looked out over vast distances in every direction. Coming down, they explored some of the small fissure craters and climbed about on tumbled lava, ankle deep in soft, silvery green reindeer moss.

"Plenty here to interest people," Tara said with satisfaction. "I shall certainly have this on the list."

Aware of the time slipping by, they left and drove along the lonely track. They had a difficult journey ahead of them, Tara knew, and she shared Jon's anxiety as he glanced at his watch.

"The sun's still high," she pointed out. "We've got a good five hours' daylight left."

"It's not darkness I'm worried about," Jon said. "Though that would make this drive virtually impossible . . . It's the rivers. The sun's been quite warm this afternoon – look how the frost has gone from the open slopes. It's been quite enough to send down a sizeable flood of meltwater. And we've got a riverbed for part of the road, just before Eldgja."

Tara said nothing. She had only been here once before and the river had been little more than a trickle. Jon glanced at her and said with a hint of impatience, "I'm not joking, Tara. The rivers might be easy enough to cross in the morning after a cold night but they can be raging torrents by afternoon. Even a big four-wheel drive tour bus would have difficulty fording them. There have been plenty of vehicles swept away because people didn't realise the danger."

He compressed his lips and concentrated grimly on his driving, while Tara sat silently beside him. Did he think she was a child? Did he think she didn't understand these things?

They arrived at the nature reserve and began the slow, wet drive along the riverbed itself. Tara clung to her seat as the wagon lurched through the water, its wheels slipping and grabbing at the pebbles and rocks beneath the surface. It was impossible for Jon to see just where they might strike a rock or plunge into a hole; his knuckles were white as he gripped the wheel, which seemed to have taken on a life of its own, twisting and jerking in his hands. His brow furrowed with concentration, he drove slowly between towering black rocks, sculpted smooth by the surging water that would almost fill the gorge after heavy rain.

After what seemed like hours, the track rose out of the river and up a steep hill. As they reached the top, Tara realised that here was a further danger: the descent on

131

the other side, smooth rock interspersed with the inevitable boulders and potholes, was also icy, and with soaked brakes Jon's task was even more difficult. He paused for a moment and she glanced at him doubtfully. He sensed her glance and gave her a challenging look. "Sure you want to bring your tourists here?" Tara looked down into the valley. "Yes, I am. Apart from Laki itself – and I realise we might not always be able to get all the way there – this is so lovely. All those hummocky hills, covered with reindeer moss, the little streams criss-crossing the valley floor and those gullies and rocks on the hillsides, which I can use to illustrate the effects of erosion. It really is a must, provided the weather's right. And we'd have a bus, that would make it easier." And a more co-operative driver, she thought.

Jon shrugged. "Well, let's hope they've got strong stomachs for travelling. A bus will lurch even more than this wagon does. Anyway, we'd better press on. That riverbed took a long time."

He put the engine into gear again and they began the slow, careful descent of the rocky track, snaking down the short, hairpin bends, skidding sometimes on loose gravel or ice, the wheel a live thing in Jon's hands, the vehicle almost dancing as it slithered rather than drove down to the valley floor to follow the staked road.

Tara let out a long sigh and realised she'd been holding her breath. She glanced at the man beside her. With his tawny hair glinting red-gold in the western sun, he looked more than ever like an ancient Viking intent on conquering a new land. She could imagine him with shield and helmet, standing tall and broad at the prow of his longship as it sailed into harbour. Settling differences with his sword, stalking proudly over this new, undiscovered land, making it his own. A leader, a man others would follow without question, a man who would inspire respect, admiration, love . . .

132

Love. There it was again, that word that kept coming unbidden into her mind. And always in association with Jon Magnusson.

But she didn't love him. She couldn't. He wasn't her type. Physically, he might attract her – and did, she admitted honestly, with those broad shoulders and narrow hips, those rugged good looks and brilliant blue eyes. But as a man, a person – no. He was far too sure of himself. Far too overbearing, too domineering.

Tara didn't want to be dominated by anyone. Mike had tried that once. But he hadn't had the personality this man had. Tara had beaten him easily. She had ignored his pleas that she should give up the opportunity of the Antarctic expedition and had gone, knowing it was the right thing for her, even though she had lost respect for Mike in the process.

But Jon Magnusson wouldn't be so easy to beat, she reflected. If it came to a showdown between them it would be a real battle. And it was a battle she didn't want to fight.

So was she *afraid* of him? Her whole being rejected the idea, yet she knew that there must be a grain of truth in it. And she knew that she didn't want to put it to the test. And if she was afraid of him – in any way at all – how could she possibly love him?

I don't love him, she told herself fiercely. I don't. I *don't*.

The tyre went down while they were looking at the Ofaerufoss waterfall.

Tara had insisted that this was something they must see. It meant a drive off the main track to reach a small parking area and then leaving the wagon in order to walk along a narrow, rocky path along the floor of the fissure, beside the tumbling river. Wide and sheltered, the walk was as pleasant as any that could be found in Scotland, she said, and her tourists would enjoy the exercise as well as the spectacular view of the waterfall itself.

"But you don't actually need to do it yourself," Jon had protested as they drove slowly along the main track. "You've seen it before, haven't you?"

"Yes, but I still need to time it from the moment we turn off the main track to the moment we come back to it. Including getting a busload of interested people along to the falls, stopping to look at things on the way, and plenty of time to explore the fall itself. It really is unique, Jon."

"I know that. But you can judge the time you need without going there. Allow some for the drive, there and back from the turning, plus an hour or so for the walk and fall. Won't that do?"

"No." Tara felt her mouth set in an obstinate line. "If I were going to do the trip like that, I'd just sit at home with the guide book. But I told Alec I'd do it properly, go to see everything on the itinerary, make sure there are parking places, suss out any possible trouble spots, that sort of thing. I have to go, Jon. I'm not missing Ofaerufoss."

"And if we get stranded?"

"We won't get stranded. It's been cold today; the glaciers won't be sending down so much meltwater. We've only got one more big river to cross, after all."

"Any stream can be a big river," he said grimly. "And Eldgja was wetter than I'd expected. And you only need *one* big river to stop you."

Tara looked at him. He was determined not to let her go to Ofaerufoss, she thought. Determined to have his own way. Well, she could be stubborn too.

"Look," she said, "this is *my* trip. You're coming along to keep an eye on me but that's not by my wish. All right, so I've been glad enough to have someone with me at times today, but that doesn't mean I'm letting you take over. I want to go to Ofaerufoss."

She caught his sideways glance. For a moment, she was aware of a battle of wills going on between them, a battle neither was willing to lose.

"Your trip?" Jon said, an edge to his voice. "You're the boss, is that it?" He paused for a moment. The turning to Ofaerufoss was in sight now. Tara watched his hands on the wheel, wondering if he would make the turn. Wondering what she would do if he didn't. What she *could* do . . . "All right," he said suddenly, and the wheel turned in his hands. "If that's the case, we'll go to Ofaerufoss. But it's your responsibility, understand? Whatever happens from now on, the buck stops with you."

"That suits me." She kept her voice cool. "I've always been prepared to take my own responsibility."

"Good." The wagon bumped its way into the wide, deep fissure, jerking as it hit rocks and holes. "But no lingering – you'll have to allow extra time for your people. We can't afford to waste a minute now. As I keep telling you, there's still a sizeable river to cross, not to mention God knows how many streams."

"Fine." Elated by her victory, Tara waited until he pulled up in the flat area that would be crowded with cars in summer. She jumped out and set off along the path. Jon would catch her up quickly enough, and she knew he was right – they had no time to waste. In fact, she was surprised that he'd agreed to stop here at all. Even after their dispute, she'd expected him to turn round in the parking space and drive straight back up the track

He came alongside her as she walked steadily along the twisting little track, leaping on and off the smaller boulders, squeezing past the larger ones. The end of the fissure could be seen ahead, a great black cliff rearing against the skyline.

And after perhaps ten or fifteen minutes they came in view of the waterfall itself.

"It really is incredible," Tara said, pausing. "That great double fall and the natural rock arch – it's the sort of thing we'd love to build and would never be able to."

"We could. It would just be a tremendous enterprise."

"And we still wouldn't get it right. Nature's a better sculptor than man could ever be."

They stood gazing at the foss, tumbling ceaselessly over the towering cliff to drop in a straight fall to the broad ledge of rock beneath. From here it spread in a white foam, to fall again in a cloud of glittering spray beneath the natural bridge that crossed in a graceful curve from one side of the lower fall to the other. It was, as Tara said, a masterpiece of natural sculpture. And it was a must for her itinerary.

"Everywhere's a must for you," Jon said tersely. "And my must is that we've got to get back to the wagon as soon as we can. You'll have to let your people climb about over there and look at the rocks, and so on, I know that. But we don't have time, so let's get going now."

"Mm. I think I'll have to split this trip in two, somehow." Tara turned reluctantly to follow him. "There's far too much to do it all in one day. You might wait a minute, though," she added aggrievedly as she watched his long legs stride away from her along the path. "I can't walk that fast and I'm not running to keep up."

"Sorry, you'll have to try." He flung the words abruptly over his shoulder. "I mean it, Tara, we're pressed for time now. There'll be no more stopping until we've got over all the main rivers and streams."

Panting, irritated, but aware that he was right, Tara stumbled after him. She was beginning to feel tired. It had been a long day and even sitting in a station wagon on Icelandic roads was an exhausting business. Each lurch of the vehicle over rocks, in and out of potholes, through rivers, meant work for muscles which were having to fight to keep the body in position. It was only now that she began to realise just how wearying it was.

Alec's clients would feel it too, she thought, even in a coach. She would have to make allowances for that . . .

"Oh, *hell!*"

Startled, Tara came round the last bend. She saw Jon standing by the wagon, his whole attitude one of exasperated fury. She paused, undecided, unwilling to put herself into the range of his anger, and then went slowly on.

"What on earth's the matter?"

He turned to her, his face dark with anger, and indicated the wagon.

"Take a look at that."

Tara looked, and with a sinking feeling realised just what he meant. The station wagon was leaning awkwardly to one side. The right hand front tyre was decidedly flat.

Jon must have seen it the moment he rounded that last bend. And known, as she knew too, just what were the implications.

He began to move, fast.

"Come on. We've got to get it changed. You'll have to help me, Tara. There's no time to play the helpless female now." He was unstrapping the spare wheel as he spoke, opening the back, dragging out the tools. Tara came forward quickly, knowing he was right, too aware of their situation to take offence at his tone. Working quickly, she did as he told her, handed him the tools he needed, rolled the damaged wheel away and brought the spare into place. This kind of work was all part of any field trip; you had to be self-sufficient if you went out into the wilds, and able to tackle any practical task to survive.

Quick and efficient though Jon was, it was twenty minutes before they had the old wheel strapped in place and were fastening their belts for the rest of the journey. Jon glanced at his watch and muttered something.

"How are we doing?" Tara asked. "We'll make it, won't we?"

"I don't know." Savagely, he thrust the engine into gear. "If we hadn't gone on that damn-fool walk . . . It was that rock we hit just after the turning. They're like knives, some of these ridges. Well, if we don't make it in time we'll just have to camp."

"*Camp*?" She stared at him. "But it's freezing. And what would we sleep in?"

"I thought you'd been on expeditions." They reached the turning, passing the offending rock, and set off along the main track. "One night in the open isn't going to kill you."

"One night with proper equipment, no. But we're totally unprepared—" She broke off, remembering the stack of baggage that Jon had stowed in the back of the wagon. In case of emergencies, he'd said, and she'd scorned him. "Well, so we're not totally unprepared," she admitted. "But it's not a specially attractive prospect, is it?"

"Which is exactly why I was so anxious to get across the rivers before they got too swollen." They came to a stream, fordable but with much more water than it would have had earlier, and Jon steered the wagon slowly across, going diagonally downstream to avoid making too high a wave. "See what I mean?"

Tara was silent. She knew he was right. They should have missed out Ofaerufoss. She could easily have assessed how long the detour would take. The truth was, she'd wanted to see it again for herself, and that was why she'd insisted on going there. If they got stranded for the night, it would be her fault and no one else's.

Worse still, it was now necessary to get the tyre repaired and that meant further delays tomorrow. And there was still so much on her itinerary, quite apart from the job she had agreed to do for Mike, which she could not put off much longer.

But the most disturbing aspect of the whole affair was the prospect of spending a night out here, stranded miles from anywhere, with Jon Magnusson. That was something she hadn't bargained for at all.

They ploughed on and with every stream they crossed Tara's spirits lifted. Surely they were going to make it. But when she said as much to Jon, he shook his head.

"We've still got the worst ahead of us. Just because the country's getting softer doesn't mean there isn't just as much risk." He glanced at the hills around them, more rolling now, with a covering of soft green turf. "At least it's a bit more hospitable for camping."

"I believe you *want* us to be stranded," Tara accused him, and he shot her a sardonic look.

"However did you guess? A night alone amongst the volcanoes and you at my mercy!" He raised shaggy brows at her expression. "Don't worry, Tara. I've a feeling you're very well able to take care of yourself. You must be, after a year on the southern ice-caps with a crowd of husky geologists. Didn't you have problems with them?"

"No, I didn't," Tara said coldly. "Most of them were married anyway, or had girlfriends at home. And I—" She stopped suddenly. Not for anything was she going to tell Jon that she'd been more or less engaged to Mike Redland. "I didn't have any problems," she ended rather lamely.

Jon gave her a curious glance, then returned his attention to the road. Tara sat beside him, watching tensely. Round the next bend, she knew, they would come in sight of the biggest of the obstructions they were likely to encounter: the main river descending from the Myrdalsjokull glacier. If this had swollen as much as the streams and rivers they had crossed so far, it would be impassable until morning.

The track twisted across another of Laki's lavafields. They came round the bend, down a last steep slope, and saw the river ahead of them.

Jon braked and the wagon came to a sudden halt.

"My God," he said softly, and Tara groaned and closed her eyes.

"I don't think," Jon said, "that I have ever seen this river so full."

Tara opened her eyes. The water was rushing down the valley as if a sluice gate had been opened. Murky white, filled with debris from the glacier, it poured across its rocky bed, shaping itself into broken waves and smooth leaping curves, twisting back on itself, splintering into flying white spray. The track led to its bank and then disappeared. It was difficult to see where it emerged on the far side, but in any case it was obvious that nobody but a madman would attempt a crossing while it was in such full spate. No vehicle, not even a coach with its great wheels and high sides, would be able to withstand the tremendous force of that roaring current.

"Well," Jon said, "it looks like a night under the stars for us, Tara."

"Isn't there anywhere else we can cross?" she asked, knowing it was a silly question.

Jon didn't even bother to answer. Instead, he drove a short distance along the riverbank to a flat, grassy ledge about twenty feet above the water. He pulled up again and switched off the engine.

"We'll camp here. The river won't reach this far." He glanced at the sky, its clear blue already beginning to take on the tinge of evening. "It's probably freezing again already, up on the glacier. There won't be much more melt coming down."

"It'll still be several hours before we see any difference though," Tara said, and he nodded.

"No use even thinking about moving till morning. Well, we'd better use the daylight to get ourselves organised." He slid out of his seat and went round to open the back of the wagon. "Help me get this gear out."

Tara did as he said. She was far from happy about the situation, but knew that there was nothing else for it. She looked around at the silent mountains, the roaring river. There was nobody in sight, nothing that even hinted at the presence of other people in the world. She felt very much alone.

She remembered Jon's words, *'a night alone amongst the volcanoes – and you at my mercy,'* and shivered suddenly. They'd been spoken flippantly enough, but had there been an undercurrent of meaning in them? She didn't really know him, after all, and he'd already kissed her several times, with obvious enjoyment. (All right, so she'd enjoyed it too, but that wasn't the point!) And only yesterday evening – though it seemed like years ago now – she'd been so swept away by his kisses that she'd invited him to her room, knowing that he'd see it as an invitation to make love. Let's be honest, she thought, I *wanted* him to make love to me. It was only later that I came to my senses. If Mike hadn't phoned . . . And she gave a wry grin at the thought that she actually had something to be grateful to Mike for.

But I don't want him to make love to me now, she thought forcibly, and gave him a sideways glance as he busied himself with the camping gear. And I especially don't want him to make me want him . . . oh, that sounded ridiculous. But he'd managed it before, hadn't he? Managed somehow to wheedle her into forgetting her fears, her antagonism. Managed to make her melt with desire in his arms, her lips quivering under his . . .

The thought brought a sharp tingle to her stomach and she turned away abruptly. For heaven's sake, she was thinking herself into it! Forget him, she thought, or at least forget what he can do to you. Keep out of arm's reach. If we just don't touch, don't let our eyes meet, it will be all right. If we just don't touch . . .

"Here," Jon said, passing her a polythene water carrier and a saucepan with a folding handle. "Set up the small stove and boil some water. We'll have a hot drink and then we'll go for a swim."

"A *swim*?"

"Certainly. There's a hot pool here, didn't you know? Might as well get some fun out of being stranded." He slanted her a devilish grin. "Don't tell me you didn't bring your swimsuit."

"No, I didn't. You never mentioned—"

"Thought you knew the area," he said laconically. "Anyway, I didn't think we'd have time today. Nor would we have," he added pointedly, and Tara blushed. "But since we're here – well, like I say, we may as well make use of the amenities." He glanced at the water carrier in her hand. "It won't pour itself into the pan."

Hastily, Tara filled the saucepan and set it on the small gas stove. She glanced at the equipment Jon had unpacked. Cooking gear, dried food, water – glacier water could be used in a real emergency, but was too full of impurities and debris to be used willingly – sleeping bags, a lamp to save the car battery, thin foam mattresses.

A tent?

She looked again. No tent.

"Where do we sleep?" she asked after a moment and Jon, who had been inspecting the river, looked round.

"In the wagon, of course."

"In the *wagon*?"

"Yes. Why not?"

"But – but there isn't room."

"Yes there is. The back seats fold down and there's ample

room." His glance was mocking. "Wide as a double bed, what more could you ask?"

"Two singles," she retorted. "Or a separate room. Why don't you carry a tent?"

"On this terrain? How would you anchor it down? This grass is growing in about two inches of soil on solid rock – you'd never get a tent peg in it. Anyway, why should I when the wagon is so roomy?" He smiled. "I don't always have guests, you know."

Tara blushed furiously. She found two mugs, spooned coffee into them, poured on boiling water and added powdered milk. The man thought of everything! And as she watched him unrolling the foam mattresses in the back of the station wagon and laying the sleeping bags out on top, she began to wonder just how planned this had been.

He couldn't have planned a puncture, of course. But even without that, she doubted if they would have reached this river in time to cross the torrent. And he could easily have found something else to delay them.

He'd allowed her to think that it was all her fault, that if they hadn't made the detour to Ofaerufoss, all would have been well. But he hadn't really made much effort to dissuade her, had he? And he had the whip hand, he was the driver. If he'd wanted to go straight past that turning, he would have. Knowing Jon Magnusson as she had learned to know him over the past few days, Tara had every reason to believe that he would have done just that. If he'd really wanted to.

If he really hadn't wanted to be stranded.

Alone amongst the volcanoes . . . with you at my mercy . . .

Chapter Eight

"So," Jon said after they had finished their coffee, "how about that swim?"

Tara gave him a reluctant glance. The idea of a swim in a hot pool was inviting enough, but alone out here with Jon Magnusson? And although she had told him, truly enough, that she hadn't brought any swimming gear, she could wear her underclothes . . . And then what? a voice asked her. Sleep naked?

While she hesitated, Jon went to the wagon and pulled out a small pack.

"Well, I'm going to anyway," he declared, and strolled off away from the river. "Join me if you like, it's up to you."

Tara watched him go and thought sadly what a waste it all was. This was a situation a good many girls would have given their eye teeth to be in. A lonely, beautiful camping site, a hot pool to swim in and a gorgeous hunk of Viking to share it all with. As a setting for a romantic interlude, it could hardly be bettered. So why wasn't she enjoying it?

It wasn't as if she found him repulsive – quite the reverse. He only had to glance at her with those brilliant blue eyes that could change so readily to ice, and her heart began to race. And when he kissed her . . .

That's it, she thought. That's what I'm scared of. When he kisses me, I just melt, I can't help it. So what's going to happen if he makes love to me?

And the answer came into her mind, revealing at last just

why she feared Jon Magnusson, why he was dangerous to
her. Why she couldn't afford to let him kiss her again, why
she dared not let him make love to her.

If Jon Magnusson makes love to me, she thought, *I'll be
his for ever. I'll never want another man. I'll be trapped for
the rest of my life.*

The knowledge was as stark as the mountains around her
and she faced it squarely. Why it should be so, she had
no idea. It surely couldn't be only because of his looks;
Tara had met plenty of good-looking men, men who were
equally magnetic, yet none of them had had this effect on
her. Neither could it be their situation, flung together in
this isolated place. Hadn't she spent plenty of time in lonely
places with other men and never experienced the slightest
twinge?

No, there was something else about Jon Magnusson,
something she couldn't explain. Something that drew her
to him, made her deeply aware of him, and yet at the same
time frightened her, so that she had to pull away again, had
to keep a safe distance between them.

I'm like the rope in a tug-of-war, she thought bemusedly.
What on earth is the matter with me?

She sat gazing out over the valley. The sun was sinking
low now, turning the sky to fire, and there was a glimpse
of the sea in the far distance, glittering like beaten copper.
Somewhere down there was Heklavik, and the errand she'd
promised to carry out for Mike. How was she going to
manage it with Jon on her tail all the time? How was she
ever going to escape him?

Tara sighed. She wondered how much longer he was
going to be in the hot pool. The thought of sliding into
hot water and just wallowing, with the sun slowly sinking
in a blaze of colour towards the sea, was becoming more and
more attractive every minute. And why was she worrying
anyway? It was only a swim, after all. Her bra and panties

were brief but perfectly respectable, no different from a bikini. Why should she let Jon Magnusson prevent her from enjoying herself?

Making a sudden decision, she jumped up and went to the station wagon for her own things. Jon had left the towel he had offered her in the back and she swung it over her shoulder and set off in the direction he had gone. She felt oddly defiant. Her fears were nonsense. So he was attractive, so what? She didn't have to let him get close to her. She didn't have to let him kiss her. She knew the dangers – all she had to do was avoid them. It was as simple as that.

The track took her past several low hills into a grassy valley where she could see steam rising from the brook that bubbled from the ground. Duckboards had been placed so that people could walk along them without damaging the vegetation, and she followed these and found herself on a wooden platform beside a series of pools linked by small, gurgling cascades.

It was exquisitely pretty. But where was Jon? And where was she supposed to undress?

A framed wire trellis on the platform was draped with what she recognised as Jon's shirt, sweater and jeans. Tara eyed them dubiously. Was this the only facility provided, an open-air 'changing room'? Well, it didn't really matter, did it? She wasn't actually going to remove all her clothes. She hung her towel beside Jon's and slipped quickly out of her own jeans and sweater.

There was still no sign of him and she hesitated, glancing up and downstream. It would be nice to be able to keep her bra and panties dry too. Perhaps he'd gone for a run. In any case, he wasn't around now and if she slid very quickly into the water . . .

Tara made up her mind. Dusk was falling anyway. Rapidly, she slipped off her remaining clothes and, shivering a little in the cold air, let herself down into the water.

It was as hot as the hottest bath she had ever taken and waist deep. With a gasp of delight she sank down until she was almost completely immersed, only her head above the water, and then swam easily across the pool into a deeper part. Here she could feel the stream itself, bringing a constant flow of fresh, hot water into the pool and she closed her eyes and wallowed luxuriously.

"So you decided to brave it after all!"

The voice sounded almost in her ear. Tara's eyes flew open and she jerked her head round to find Jon about a yard away from her in the water, his eyes glinting.

Tara spluttered. "Where did you come from? I looked all around – I couldn't see you anywhere—"

He indicated with his head, tawny hair darkened to a deep auburn by the water.

"I was having a warm shower under that waterfall – it drops down into the next pool." His eyes moved over her shoulders. "Did you find a swimsuit after all?"

Tara remembered suddenly that she was naked. Automatically, she crossed her arms over her breasts, wondering just how much he could see below the clear water. She glanced down and to her dismay realised that he was naked too. And that the water was altogether *too* clear. Aware that her face and neck – and probably a good deal more of her – were scarlet, she turned quickly away.

Jon laughed. "So you're a water nymph! Well, what does that make me – a satyr?" Damn him, she could hear the grin in his voice. "And why not?" he purred. "It's the only way to bathe, don't you agree? Where's the sense in getting clothes deliberately wet, even if that is what they're designed for?"

"I wouldn't have come if I'd realised – if I'd thought you—"

"If you'd thought I was bathing nude too? Come off it, Tara." There was a brisk scepticism in his voice and she

147

turned back indignantly. "You knew perfectly well I was here. Didn't you, now?"

"I couldn't see you anywhere. I thought you might have – might have—" She floundered to a stop, realising just how muddled and illogical her thoughts had been, but Jon took them up swiftly.

"Thought I'd gone for a run, perhaps? With *nothing on*? You must have seen my clothes on the platform."

"Yes, but I didn't know you were – didn't have swimming things—"

"Which makes no difference to the fact that you decided to bathe naked." There was a different note in his voice and she glanced at him, startled. What were they doing, she thought wildly, standing here in a pool of hot water in the mountains, arguing about motives? But before she could find any answer, he was continuing, his voice crisp. "Look, Tara, ever since we met you've been playing me like a fish on a hook. Or trying to . . . A little tug to bring me to your side, a bit of play with the net and then – whoosh, I'm out in the cold again, tossed back into the water like a minnow, not worth catching. Why do you do it? What's it all about?"

Tara stared at him. "*I've* been playing . . . ? You're out of your mind. I've been doing nothing of the sort. It's you—"

"*Me*?"

"Yes, you!" Forgetting her nakedness, she came closer, the hot water lapping at her shoulders. "You've never missed an opportunity to remind me that you're a big macho male. You're either putting me down, treating me like a bimbo or – or *kissing* me!" She heard her voice rise with indignation and stopped, exasperated. Why did it have to go shrill just when she needed it to be most commanding? They never managed to teach you that at assertiveness classes. And he was *laughing* at her, blast him. His eyes were glittering with mirth. Oh, if only he weren't so damned *attractive!*

"Poor Tara," Jon said, his voice shaking. "You are having a rough time, aren't you? A qualified geologist, here on a serious mission and having to be accompanied everywhere you go by this chauvinistic Icelander, who won't even take you seriously. It's a shame."

"Look, I know you're laughing at me," Tara said. "You needn't bother to try to keep a straight face. Just let it go. Have yourself a good time. Why should I care? I'm going to apply for a job in a television sitcom next. Or maybe as stooge for some clever male comedian."

"Oh no," Jon said, his lips twitching maddeningly. "There's no male comedian on earth could match you, Tara, my love."

The last words hung in the air between them. To Tara's startled eyes, Jon's expression seemed to alter as they were spoken, almost as he were hearing them for the first time, tilting his head as if to listen, and his eyes grew wide and dark as he glanced at Tara.

Disturbed, she stepped away from him and stumbled on a rock. With a splash and a flurry of broken water, she righted herself and then decided to keep on swimming. At least it took her away from him, away from the scrutiny of those blue eyes and the sudden constraint between them.

The temperature of the water varied as the current from the stream ran through it, dropping as it met the colder water that was artificially pumped in to make the pool safe for bathing. Even with the addition of cold water, there were spots that were too hot for comfort, and she swam carefully, heading slowly towards the waterfall that dropped into the next pool, where Jon had said he had been having his shower.

It really was a delightful experience to be bathing here, she thought, and one that ought to be shared with someone you loved, or at least liked and trusted. And it would have been very nearly perfect if she could have felt that way towards Jon. But he didn't trust her, did he? He'd made that very clear. And he even seemed to blame her for the tension between them, the sexual awareness that hung in the air.

And that wasn't fair. Didn't it take two?

Yes, it does, she thought, and realised that she must therefore accept her own responsibility. She'd wanted him to kiss her. She'd wanted him to make love to her. It hadn't all been on his side.

She turned to see where he was. He was treading water a few yards away, watching her gravely through the deepening twilight, and she met his eyes and knew that the same thoughts had been going through his mind. The same acceptance of responsibility.

"Jon . . ." she said hesitantly, and he came closer.

"I know, Tara. We've both been playing games, haven't we?" His eyes were almost purple now, reflecting the darkened colour of the sky. "Why is that, do you suppose? Why do we do this – keep coming closer, only to draw away again? What are we afraid of?"

She stared at him. He was so close to her now that she could almost feel the brush of his skin beneath the water.

"You feel it too?" she breathed, and he nodded.

"I've never felt anything like this before." His voice was low and ragged. "I thought I was in love once – but it was never like this." He reached out almost tentatively and laid his hands on her shoulders. Tara moved towards him as if magnetised, drawn against the current of the water. "You terrify me, Tara," he murmured, looking down into her upturned face. "You seem to hold so much – a world in your eyes, in the hands you hold out to me. And yet I know that if I try to take that world, you'll demand more from me than I've ever given anyone in my life. More than I'm sure I have to give." His arms were close around her now and she could feel her breasts softening against his chest, the length of his body against hers. "Suppose I fail you, Tara?" he whispered against her mouth. "Suppose my macho act breaks down? What happens to us then?"

She shook her head, hardly able to believe what was happening, what he was saying, hardly knowing how to respond. Did she want this – this urgent need, this overwhelming desire for another human being, this invasion of her senses, her body, her mind? Was this the fear he felt too, the fear of giving herself up completely to another person?

"Jon, I don't know," she whispered as his lips brushed hers. "I don't know . . . I've never . . . I can't . . ." But her jumbled thoughts were lost in the kiss, whirling away from her into outer space, and she could only close her eyes and part her lips and let him hold her, his fingers stroking gently over her skin, touching her breasts with a gentleness that was somehow unexpected, slipping with featherlike lightness down her back to her waist, her thighs . . .

"Oh, Tara, Tara," he groaned, breaking away suddenly and then pulling her hard against him. "What's happening? What are you doing to me? Do you know? Do you have any idea?"

She shook her head, leaning her face against his shoulder. The water was like silk, flowing around their bodies as if they were part of it, as if the country itself caressed them with its magic.

Jon stirred against her and murmured, "Look. Look up, Tara."

Almost reluctantly, she opened her eyes and lifted her head away from his shoulder. And then gasped in sheer wonder.

The sky had fully darkened now, the stars a thickly clustered mass of bright needlepoints. But they were dwarfed and dimmed by the brilliant display of Northern Lights that had spread unnoticed over the entire dome of the heavens, turning them into an upturned bowl of glorious, changing colour. Unpolluted by any artifical lights, they made a majestic, silent symphony of colour against the backdrop of the mountains. And when she looked about her, Tara saw that they were reflected in the water that lapped her skin, so that she and Jon seemed bathed in a world of slowly moving iridescence, enclosed in an eternal rainbow that danced in courtly saraband about their naked bodies.

"It's magic," she whispered. "This whole country is magic. I could believe in anything at this moment, Jon – elves, fairies, trolls, elemental beings of any kind. They have to be real in a place where this can happen."

"Could you believe in me?" he asked softly, and she nodded. The warm water had soaked away all her doubts, melted all resistance. In this world of colour and silence and steaming pools, everything was possible, and nothing could be denied.

"Then let's seal our belief," he said, and lifted her in his arms. "Come out of the water, Tara. Come back to the station wagon and let's warm ourselves with our love. Let's live this magic night as it ought to be lived – add our own form of beauty to the beauty that's all around."

She could not speak. Together, they climbed out of the pool and dried themselves with their towels. They slipped into their clothes and walked hand in hand back along the duckboards, their way lit by the kaleidoscope of colour that blazed above them. Still warmed by the water, they came to the station wagon and Jon opened the back for Tara to creep inside, onto the bed of foam and feather that he had made earlier.

"Let's unzip these bags," he murmured, "and make them into one. Not that we'll need them yet. We're going to generate our own private volcano here, you and I." He drew her down against him and slid her clothes from her tingling body. "Oh, Tara, Tara, you're magic tonight, do you know that? You've enchanted me, woven a web of spells about me so that I don't know what's real any more, only that you're real, that you and I are real, that the rest of the world out there is the illusion and this, *this* the reality."

He ran his hands gently but rapidly over her body and she shivered and almost cried out. She felt the unique sensation of her skin against his, the warmth of living flesh touching her own, setting her on fire. With a sudden surge of desire, she knew that she wanted him, that nothing could stand in the way of their consummation. She pressed against him, moaning as his fingers brought new and exquisite sensations, her desire now almost unbearable, pulsing through her, driving her lips to seek his, her hands to caress his body, her fingers trembling as she let them move over his heated skin.

"Jon," she whispered, "Jon . . ." And her voice begged him, as her eyes, hands and body pleaded, for the release that they both so desperately needed. It was too soon, she knew, too quick, but for this first time, it had to be so. Later, there would be time for a more leisurely lovemaking . . . time to explore, to tease, to enjoy . . .

Jon twisted himself above her. He looked down into her eyes and she nodded, unable to see his face but knowing what question was there. And then she cried out again as he touched her again, gently and then with increasing force until at last she received him and her body joined his in a smooth rhythm that was older than time, the rhythm from which all life must spring. And then, as she lay in his arms, her mind soaring towards the stars, she opened her eyes and saw from the windows of the station wagon the colours that danced in the sky. And her heart exploded with all those colours, sending her spinning to join them, to be a part of them; to be one with the glory of the heavens.

Morning came softly after the passion of the night, and the sun shone through the wagon's windows at the two who lay entwined inside. Tara stirred, yawned, rubbed her eyes and turned over. She felt the warmth of Jon's body beside her.

Jon! In an instant she was awake, staring in disbelief at the man who still lay asleep on his back, one arm across her waist. The memory of the night came flooding back and heat coursed through her body, but whether it was the heat of renewed desire or total embarrassment she hardly knew. A tumult of feelings surged inside her and she drew away, her mind in panic, her heart thudding wildly.

What on earth had she done? After all she had told herself, all the decisions she'd made, all her determination not to get involved . . . She hadn't even *tried* to resist. She'd allowed herself to be swept away by the seductively warm water of the hot pool, the isolation, the glory of the Northern Lights, the nearness of Jon and the attraction that she could no longer deny. She'd let a sudden flame of desire sweep away all her reason.

And now, as she'd known and feared all along, she was committed.

Propped on one elbow, Tara looked down at the sleeping man. She let her eyes move slowly over his face, lingering caressingly on the tawny brows, the straight shape of his nose, the firm lips. Those lips had touched her own, had roamed over her face, her neck, her body, knew every part of her . . . she felt her face burn at the recollection. What was she to say when he woke?

And how was she going to live the rest of her life, knowing that this night had made her his for ever? Knowing that for him it had been nothing but an enjoyable way to pass the time . . .

She gave a soft moan and dropped her head on one hand.

At her movement, Jon woke. He opened his eyes and stared sleepily at her, then she saw memory dawn in his eyes as it must have done in hers. But there seemed to be no confusion in his reaction. With a slow smile, he reached out and slid a hand around her waist, gathering her close.

"Jon . . . no . . ."

"Why not?" he murmured against her hair. "I haven't exhausted you, have I?"

"No. Yes. *No.* Oh – I don't know what I'm saying. I don't know what I'm *doing.* What happened to us last night, Jon?" She stared at him. "Please, no funny answers." She tried to pull away. "It wasn't meant to happen. I'd thought it all out, made up my mind—"

"So you knew it was possible. If not probable." His eyes narrowed as he gazed at her. "Why did it matter so much, Tara?"

She stared at him in shock, even though it was exactly the reaction she'd expected from him. But she couldn't let him know just how much it mattered. Instead, she forced a laugh and said, "Of course it matters. I don't sleep with just any man I happen to be stranded with. A girl likes to be able to choose, you know."

An odd expression crossed Jon's face and he let her go abruptly. "Of course. I'd forgotten we were into the Nineties now. We've moved on a bit from general permissiveness, people hopping into bed as easily as pouring a cup of coffee, but women still consider themselves liberated. And if you enjoy a fling, why not? It doesn't always have to mean something – does it?"

There was an undertone to his words that she didn't understand. As if he were asking her something else, something his words covered up. But she couldn't understand it, could only take the question at face value.

"Depends who you are, I suppose," she said as lightly as possible. "To some people, it's no more than that. To others it's a – a statement."

"And was that what it was for you, Tara?" he asked

155

quietly. "A statement?" He paused fractionally, then added, "A statement of what?"

There was a long pause. Tara sought frantically for words, knowing she could never tell him the truth. She had no doubt as to how he would react. With incredulous disbelief that any woman in the Nineties would consider one brief sexual encounter a commitment of any kind? The whole thing would be too embarrassing to bear, even worse than it was already. Yet at the same time, she couldn't let him think that it was no more than a fling, that it was her habit to behave that way with any attractive man she happened to find herself alone with.

So what *was* she to say?

Her eyes filling with sudden tears, she turned her head away and stared out of the window. She was aware of Jon watching her, even more aware of his fingers caressing her waist, and suddenly she could bear it no longer. With an exclamation, she kicked herself as far away from him as she could get in the confines of the station wagon, and searched amongst the tumbled sleeping bags for her clothes. Snatching up her jeans and shirt, she pushed the door open and scrambled out, thankful that she was now more or less hidden from his gaze. Having him watch her dress was something she could not tolerate. With shaking fingers, she dragged on her jeans and then pulled her shirt and sweater over her head.

Jon slid round to the door and peered out. He looked almost unbearably attractive, his blond hair tousled from sleep, and Tara turned her eyes determinedly away.

"What in hell's the matter, Tara?" he demanded. "So we had a volcanic night together – it doesn't have to be a big deal, does it? Not if you don't want—"

Tara whipped round and glared at him. The chill of humiliation was cooling her body, still warm from his loving. How could she have let him do it? How could she have *asked* for it? For she knew that she had. The magic of the night, the spectacular display of the Aurora, had swept her away. But being angry with herself didn't help; she had to let it out on him.

"A volcanic night!" she hissed. "Yes, that's just what you intended, wasn't it? Didn't you say so when we were first stranded here? 'A night amongst the volcanoes, and you at my mercy.' You meant it to happen all along. You *meant* us to get stranded. You knew I couldn't – couldn't—" Her voice broke and she turned away to hide the tears. He'd known she couldn't resist him. He'd already kissed her, and he knew.

Jon stared at her, then reached back for his own jeans. A moment later, his torso still bare, he stood beside her.

"Look, Tara, if that's the way you feel, let's just forget it, shall we? Obviously we both made a mistake. I'm sorry – I thought it was pretty good myself." She knew his eyes were on her, but she couldn't look up, couldn't meet them. "More than pretty good, as it happens. And I'd like to think you'd enjoyed it too and that we could both remember it with some pleasure. But if you'd rather not . . . Okay, we pretend it never happened. Does that suit you?"

Pretend it never happened! she thought. When it will haunt me to the end of my life? But Jon didn't know that, and neither must he. She must never, never let him suspect how it had affected her. Never let him suspect what she now knew – what she had known all along but refused to admit. That she loved him.

"No," she said in a low voice. "No, it doesn't suit me at all. I'd rather it had never happened. But we can't alter that, can we? So I don't have much choice but to pretend. But I'll tell you one thing." She faced him squarely, hiding the pain in her heart. "It's never going to happen again."

"Never again," he said quietly.

Tara turned away. She walked to the edge of the river and gazed down at the water. The flow had slowed during the

157

night and they would have no trouble in fording it, nor any of the other streams they would encounter before reaching the ring road.

Never again to lie in Jon's arms, never again to feel his fingertips moving over her skin, to open her lips to his kisses, to slide her own hands over his body and feel him harden with desire for her. Never again to experience that explosion of stars, of light and colour, of sheer soaring love . . .

I do love him, she thought miserably. And all he feels for me is – well, attraction. A 'fling.' Something 'pretty good' to be remembered 'with pleasure.' No more than a way of passing the time.

But for Tara, it was something that had changed the course of her life. And now, just as she had feared, she was bound.

Bound to him for ever.

Chapter Nine

When Tara returned to the station wagon, Jon had made coffee and put together some sandwiches. Silently, she accepted the drink but shook her head at food. It would have tasted like ashes in her mouth. She leaned against the side of the vehicle, holding her coffee mug in both hands and staring out over the landscape. It was as bleak as her heart.

Jon came and stood beside her. She kept her head averted but knew that he was glancing at her. In a moment or two he would speak. If she tried to answer him she knew she would break down in tears. To avoid it, she turned abruptly away and moved a few yards off to sit on a rock.

"Look," he said after a few minutes, "we can't go on like this, Tara. We're going to have to talk."

"Talk about what?" Her voice was brittle, cracking like faulty ice, but at least she hadn't begun to cry. Yet. She stared miserably at the stony ground, her throat aching.

"About us. About – oh, about *anything*." He waved his hand helplessly. "We've still got quite a way to go, Tara. We can't pretend we're not together. I can't just disappear."

If only you could, she thought. If only one of those elves we've been talking about could spirit you away. It doesn't have to be for seven years. Just a few hours would do, long enough for me to get back to civilisation. Long enough for me to get away from you, from everything that reminds me of you, from Iceland itself . . .

159

But she couldn't do that. She hadn't even half completed her mission here. She couldn't leave Iceland until she'd carried out the job for Alec. Neither could she neglect Mike's errand. Of the two, it was, after all, the more vital.

"Look," Jon said again, his tone striving to be reasonable, "if you like I'll try to arrange for someone else to complete the trip with you. Someone else from the University, or maybe from the tourist offices. Maybe that'd be the best thing for both of us."

Maybe it would, she thought, but at the same time she knew that if Jon left her the ache in her heart would be even more painful than it was now. And yet only minutes ago, she'd been wishing he could be spirited away . . . What was wrong with her, for heaven's sake?

If this was what they called love, she'd rather be without it. Instead of which, was she doomed to live like this for the rest of her life? Longing for him, aching for him, and knowing it could never be . . .

"Would you like me to do that?" he asked, his voice oddly gentle. "Arrange for someone else?"

It would be the best thing, she knew. The most sensible thing. The *right* thing. And yet . . .

"Oh, do whatever you think best!" How could her voice sound so waspish, when she was hurting so much inside? How could she sound so aggrieved, so irritated, as if she really didn't care, as if the whole shambles were no more than an annoyance? But the pain in her throat seemed to have just that effect on her voice and there was nothing she could do about it. And maybe it was just as well. Hadn't she already known that she couldn't bear Jon to realise just how she felt? "Let's just get away from here, can we? The river's low enough now, surely."

Jon glanced away at the water. It was rippling gently past, the tumbling waves of yesterday gone. The cold night had refrozen the snout of the glacier from which the meltwater

160

flowed and in comparison with last night's deluge there was little more than a trickle. But by afternoon it would be in spate once more.

"Yes, we can make it easily now," he said briefly. "So as you say, let's get going. Sure you don't want a sandwich? Okay, I'll put them in the door pocket so they're handy if you do get peckish."

Quickly, he rearranged the equipment at the back of the wagon. Tara watched as he rolled up the sleeping bags, unavoidably reminded of the night they had spent there together. The tenderness, the passion . . . She snapped her mind away, turning to stare determinedly across the sandur towards the sea and when Jon had finished she climbed in without a word.

They were on the main road by ten and Tara drew a breath of relief. But instead of taking the turning towards Reykjavik, Jon directed the vehicle in the opposite direction. With a jerk, Tara sat up sharply in her seat.

"Where are you going?"

"Where do you think?" His mouth was set in the uncompromising line which had become familiar to her and which she knew meant an argument – an argument she was by no means sure to win.

And by no means sure to lose either, she thought angrily. Did this man think he could dominate her still, after all that had happened?

Or . . . *because* of all that had happened . . . ?

"We're supposed to be going to Reykjavik," she answered tersely. "For you to arrange for someone else to come with me, I thought."

"But I didn't realise you'd agreed to that." His tone was infuriatingly bland. "You shrugged it off, said to do whatever I thought best. And—"

"You surely don't think it best to go on as we have been!"

161

"Not as we have been, no." He glanced at her and she saw that his eyes were serious. "On consideration, I thought it best to give it one more chance. To give *us* one more chance."

"One more chance for what?" she demanded suspiciously, and he sighed.

"One more chance to behave like civilised human beings, Tara. One more chance to get that chip off your shoulder, whatever it is. Because behind that prickly manner I occasionally get a glimpse of someone I could get along with very well. More than a glimpse sometimes," he added softly.

Tara was silent. Once again, she felt that if she tried to answer him, when he had spoken so gently, she would burst into tears. And that was something she couldn't let happen. Whatever he did, whether he took her in his arms to comfort her, or simply shrugged her tears off as female hysterics, it could only make things worse. It was better, she thought miserably, when they were quarrelling. When they were hostile. That was the only way she could stay in control.

Jon waited a moment, as if to give her a chance to answer. Then he set his mouth once again in that grim line and accelerated. The station wagon surged ahead with a sudden burst of speed, still heading away from Reykjavik.

"So where *are* we going?" Tara demanded at last, her voice higher than she would have liked but at least reasonably under control.

"You forget," he said tersely, "we have a tyre to be repaired. That has to be done before we think about anything else. And there's something else I've decided—"

"*You've* decided?" Tara seized his words almost with gratitude for the opportunity they gave her to let her feelings out in anger. "Just when did this become *your* trip? All right, so we've got to get the tyre repaired, but there are garages in

Reykjavik, I'm sure. We certainly don't need to head in the opposite direction. So if you don't mind, you can just turn round right now and take me where *I* want to go!"

"Such authority!" Jon marvelled. "Tara, has anyone ever told you that when you're angry you look quite—"

"Oh, for heaven's sake," she groaned, "not that old chestnut. No, Jon, nobody *has* ever told me I look beautiful when I'm angry. Because I don't. I look awful. And don't try to distract me."

"I wasn't going to say that, actually," he murmured. "'Regal' was the word I had in mind. Snapping out your commands like a queen – the Red Queen, to be precise." He grinned at her outraged expression. "I'm expecting to hear you say 'Off with his head!' at any minute."

"Believe me," Tara said, "if I had an axe, I'd do it myself. With the greatest pleasure. Now will you *please* turn this car round and take me to Reykjavik."

Jon shook his head. "Sorry. No can do. But you don't have to worry, Tara. I know a very good little garage that will have the tyre repaired in no time. And it happens to be somewhere that I know you want to visit. So nothing will be lost, will it? Reykjavik isn't going to go away. It'll still be there tomorrow or the next day."

Tara stared at him suspiciously. "Somewhere I want to go? But there aren't any towns on my agenda."

"Oh, but there are." Jon took his eyes off the long straight road and gave her a slanting, enigmatic glance. "Didn't you say you wanted to go to Heklavik?"

The little town lay in a rocky bay, with a sandy beach sloping down to the sea. With green cliffs rising on either side, it could have been in Devonshire, Tara thought as Jon drove into the main street. Only the broad stretch of sandur beyond the cliffs and the white caps of the glaciers inland were reminders that Heklavik was actually in Iceland.

"What a pretty place," she said as Jon braked and pulled up outside a large white house with a red roof. "But I thought we were going to a garage?"

"I shall be. Just as soon as I've dropped you and the luggage off here." He opened his door and jumped to the ground. "Come on, Tara. The quicker we get unloaded, the quicker I can get this fixed."

Bewildered, she climbed out and stood looking at the building outside which they had stopped. "But this isn't a hotel."

"Should it be?" He heaved out her backpack. "Do you normally stay in a hotel when you go back to your home town?"

Home town? But of course – hadn't he told her he'd grown up in Heklavik? Somehow Tara had forgotten that. "Do you mean to say this is where you live?"

"Where my parents live, and where I grew up, yes." He glanced towards the house. "Looks as if they're in the back of the house, that's if they're in. But never mind, I've got a key." Heaving up some of the bags, he set off up the drive and round the side of the big house. "Bring some of those things, Tara, could you?"

Tara stared at him. Hastily, she gathered up a few of the bags and followed him before she realised quite what she was doing. Bother it! Did she *always* have to be running after him?

"You're not going to leave me here by myself, are you?" she demanded, seeing him unlock the door. "Suppose someone comes in – your father or mother—"

"Suppose they do? They won't bite you."

"But they won't know who I am—"

"So tell them," he suggested patiently, and led her inside. "Look, you can find your own way around, make some coffee, find something to eat if you're hungry. I'll get the wagon down to the garage and be back as soon as the job's done. Sorry to rush you, Tara, but Kristjan has this afternoon off and he'll have shut up shop if I don't get there soon." He gave her an exasperated glance. "You don't have to look so scared, for God's sake! I'm not leaving you in a lion's den. My parents are quite human, believe it or not."

So how come they produced a son like you? Tara thought, but she had no time to say what was in her mind. Jon had swept out of the door before she could open her mouth and the next minute she heard the sound of the station wagon's engine start up and then fade into the distance.

Tara stood in the middle of the kitchen, feeling rather breathless. Their arrival had been so quick, so hurried, that she had the feeling part of her hadn't actually got here yet, that she was still out on the road, travelling in the station wagon with Jon. And she didn't like the idea of being in someone else's house without their knowledge.

Well, Jon had seemed to think it would be all right. And he'd told her to make some coffee. She could certainly do with a hot drink. She'd had nothing since that mug of coffee Jon had made by the river early that morning. Cautiously, she began to look around.

The kitchen, bright and sparkling in the Icelandic fashion, was little different from other kitchens she had been in, and she soon found a coffee-maker and filled it with water. Coffee too was to hand, and while the water was heating she went to look for the bathroom.

It was certainly a very pleasant house, she reflected. Spacious and comfortable with gleaming floors and attractive carpets. There was a good deal of polished wood, which she knew was expensive in this country of few trees, and some interesting pictures on the walls. Attracted by these, she found herself in a large lounge, with big, squashy armchairs and sofas. She was just about to go back to the kitchen when her attention was caught by a group of photographs on a shelf.

Donna Baker

Feeling guiltily curious, Tara went over to look at them. Family photos always interested her; she liked to compare the faces she knew with the ones she didn't, guessing what the various relationships were, looking for likenesses and gaining some insight into the family by the photographs they displayed.

Jon's family seemed to be larger than she would have expected. The big, fair-haired man was obviously his father, while the small redheaded woman must be his mother. Tara remembered him telling her his mother was Scots, and he must have gained some of his colouring from her. There were two other young men as well, brothers, she guessed, and a girl who was probably his sister.

They all looked rather nice and the photos showed them enjoying themselves together: swimming in hot pools, climbing around the snout of a glacier and apparently making toast in a steaming fumerole on top of a volcano. Their faces were invariably alight with laughter and Jon looked younger and happier than she had ever seen him.

She felt a pang in her heart, remembering the moments when she and Jon had been in such accord, when they had looked into each other's eyes and found real contact. Why had it all gone so horribly wrong? Was it all her fault? Had she got things distorted, let her own problems come between them?

Her eyes moved slowly over the pictures, looking for Jon in each one. And then she gasped and caught her breath.

There was one picture of Jon alone. Except for the girl who stood beside him. He had his arm around her shoulders and they were laughing into the camera. And there was something in the way they stood, their closeness, their obvious happiness, that told Tara they were in love.

Well, why shouldn't they be? Why shouldn't Jon have a girlfriend, a fiancée even?

166

Except that he'd made love to Tara less than twenty-four hours ago. And because the girl in the picture was Heather . . .

"Hallo? Who's there?"

Tara whirled round guiltily. The voice had called out in Icelandic, and before she could answer its owner was in the room, staring at Tara in astonishment.

Tara recognised her at once from the photographs. Small, bright-eyed, redhaired – she had to be Jon's mother. But just in case she wasn't, she answered also in Icelandic, stepping forward and holding out her hand at the same time.

"Mrs Magnusson?" Did they use that form? For the life of her, she couldn't remember, yet it was a piece of knowledge as basic as that of knowing that Jon must be named Magnusson after his father. "I'm sorry about this. I came with Jon, but he's had to go and get a tyre mended. He left me here to make coffee . . ." Her Icelandic was stumbling and she went on in English. "I'm sorry, it all sounds very muddled. My name's Tara Hansen," she finished lamely.

"Jon's always doing something unexpected," the older woman said, her eyes glinting with laughter. "Leaving someone here to make coffee while he goes to get a tyre mended sounds exactly like him. But surely you're Scottish?"

"Yes, that's right. And so are you – Jon told me." She glanced round, feeling guilty again. "I really am sorry about my being here. I shouldn't have come in, but I had to find the bathroom and—"

"And it's always intriguing to explore a house in a foreign country," Jon's mother finished for her. "It's all right, I'd have done exactly the same. And my name's Shona, by the way." She shook Tara's hand and gave her a friendly smile. "But why don't we go back to the kitchen

167

now and make that coffee? The water must be just about boiling."

Tara followed her, feeling relieved that she hadn't taken offence at finding a stranger roaming around her house, and soon they were settled at the kitchen table with mugs of coffee while Tara explained what she was doing in Iceland and why Jon was accompanying her.

"You mean he's having to be a sort of minder?" his mother exclaimed. "Poor you – I shouldn't imagine he was at all keen on that job. And when Jon isn't keen on something, he does tend to let everyone else know it!"

"Well, he isn't any less keen than I was," Tara confessed. "But he's certainly carried out his assignment. There'd be no chance of my doing anything that might put Iceland at any kind of risk, even if I wanted to."

Shona laughed. "I can imagine! Jon's passionately in love with his country." Her smiled faded a little. "And a good thing too. A man needs to be passionately in love with something." There was an odd note in her voice and Tara glanced at her curiously. Was she saying that Jon had no other passions? And then her face burned as she remembered the night they had shared, but that wasn't something she could tell Jon's mother about.

And what of the photograph she'd seen in the other room? Jon and Heather together, their arms about each other, laughing? When had Jon and Heather known each other? And why had nobody – Mike, Heather, Jon himself – ever mentioned it?

"Have some more coffee," Shona offered. "And then tell me some more about this holiday agency. It sounds fascinating. Do you really think your friend will be doing trips to Peru and Thailand? I've always wanted to go there."

Tara nodded, trying to keep her mind on the conversation. "I'm sure he will. He's really keen and I think he'll make a success of it." She described some of Alec's other projects and Shona began to ask details about inoculations and other precautions. It sounded as though she was really serious. They discussed holidays in general and then Shona said a little wistfully, "Now tell me how my beloved Scotland is getting along without me. I haven't been back yet this year and I miss it sorely. Whereabouts do you come from? We might even have friends in common."

For a few minutes they talked about Scotland, and then Tara hesitated and said, "I hope you don't mind – I was looking at your family photos when I was in the other room. And I saw one of Jon with a girl . . ." She felt her cheeks colour and glanced down, sure that her feelings must be plain on her face. "I didn't know he was engaged."

A shadow crossed Shona's face. "Heather. And no, he wouldn't have mentioned her. He never does." She sighed. "Though it would be better if he could only talk—" She stopped suddenly as the station wagon sounded outside and after a moment Jon came through the door. His glance swept over them and Tara met his eyes briefly and then looked down again. What had Shona been about to say? What had happened between Jon and Heather?

"So you've met." His voice was terse. "I suppose Tara's been telling you all about the wonderful Experience Holidays."

"She has, and they do sound wonderful." Shona sounded quite unbothered by his curtness, but then she was his mother. "I'll probably go on some myself . . . And if that's the way you greet your mother after not having set foot in the house for two months, Jon, I'll be thinking I missed teaching you your manners."

"Sorry." He bent and kissed the top of his mother's head. "How are you? Has Tara told you we'll be staying a night or two? There's something she wants to look at here in Heklavik."

"Really?" Shona turned and looked at Tara. "You didn't

169

ion that. Are you thinking of bringing your tours here, then?"

"No – at least, I don't think so." Tara sent Jon a murderous glare. "It's something else, something a friend asked me to check. But I can't ask you to put me up," she added quickly. "I wouldn't dream of imposing on you. I can go to the hotel."

"Nonsense!" Shona exclaimed. "You'll do no such thing. If there's anyone more hospitable than a Scot, it's an Icelander, and as a bit of both now, I'd be mortally offended if you didn't stay with us. I know that's what Jon intended anyway, isn't it, Jon? Otherwise he would never have brought you," she ended without giving Jon a chance to answer. "And if you've finished your coffee, I'll take you up to your room this minute, and no more argument."

She got up from the table and Tara rose more slowly. As she followed Shona from the kitchen, she passed close to Jon. She paused for a moment, looking up into his eyes, trying to read their expression and wondering just what was in his mind.

But there was no hint in Jon's face as to what he might be feeling. No clue in the dark blue eyes that looked down into hers. And she found herself thinking instead of the night she had spent in his arms – the night they had agreed would never be referred to again. The night that would haunt her for the rest of her life.

What was going on behind those dark eyes, beneath the fiery hair, in the heart that had beaten so strongly against hers? What emotions seethed beneath that cool surface, like the molten lava that simmered, waiting to erupt from beneath the deep, cold ice of a glacier?

It was growing dark when they escaped at last from the house and walked down through the village towards the bay. The sky was clear, stars already beginning to prickle

170

in the deepening blue, and Tara guessed that there would be another display of the Northern Lights later.

Behind them, they left a family party which had hastily convened as soon as it was known that Jon was at home. His brothers had arrived with their families and his sister, who still lived at home, had set to with enthusiasm to help her mother prepare a gigantic meal. Tara, embarrassed, had once again suggested going to a hotel, but her protests had been quickly shouted down and the brothers vied for the honour of sitting next to her and practising their already excellent English.

There had been no time to talk with Jon, and indeed she had no idea what she was going to say to him when they were alone once more. It was difficult to remember even what footing they had been on when they had arrived here – barely speaking, surely – yet with all this warmth and gaiety surrounding them it was impossible to remember just why there had been such hostility between them. Impossible not to share the jokes that had flown about the big supper table, laughing with the rest of them and catching each other's eyes in mutual amusement.

Now, Tara felt confused and uncertain. Were they still at loggerheads, or had they somehow been reconciled? And what difference would it make anyway? She would be going home soon, leaving Iceland. It was unlikely that they'd ever meet again.

The thought stabbed sharp as a needle in her heart.

"You're very quiet," Jon said, and she jumped. So deep in thought had she been, she'd almost forgotten he was by her side.

"I was just thinking what a pretty place this is," she said not quite truthfully, although she had expressed the thought earlier. "Look at that stretch of sand on the other side of the bay and those rock stacks in the water. In England, this would be a real honeypot for holidaymakers."

She realised too late just what she'd said. She didn't have to look at him to know that his face had darkened, nor touch him to know that his body had stiffened with anger. But this time she wasn't prepared to let him misunderstand. Since arriving in Heklavik and meeting his family, she had realised that there had been too many misunderstandings already and that they were her fault as much as his.

"Look, I don't have any intention of bringing tourists here," she said quickly. "Not the bucket-and-spade brigade, anyway. I mean that, Jon."

He stopped and looked down at her. They were standing by the edge of the sea now, in the shadow of a rock. She could just see the glimmer of the stars reflected in his eyes.

"Do you really, Tara? Do you really mean it? Because I won't see Heklavik spoilt, you know. I'd do anything to prevent that."

"You won't have to do anything at all," she said gently, and laid her hands on his shoulders. She felt him quiver under her touch, felt the shiver pass across her own skin, and longed suddenly to be in his arms again. A warm tingle of desire woke inside her and spread through her body. Her lips parted, her eyes half closed and she swayed towards him.

But Jon did not respond. Instead, he put his own hands up to hers and caught her wrists, holding her away from him. He looked down as if searching her face in the dusk and she knew that he still didn't trust her. There was no reason why he should. Hadn't she consistently refused to tell him the truth about her wish to visit Heklavik?

Now that she was here, she could understand his feeling for the village. His home was here, his family lived here still, he must have friends . . . Of course he wouldn't want to see it spoilt by tourism. And she knew that she had spoken the truth when she'd denied wanting to use it for Alec's tours.

But was there any real reason why she couldn't have told him why she'd wanted to come?

It was only at Mike's insistence that she'd kept her reasons secret, she realised. And Jon had said to her once that she couldn't expect him to trust her if she wasn't open with him. She hadn't been open because *she* hadn't trusted *him*. Yet what reason had he given her for that lack of trust? None at all. It had been all Mike Redland's doing. She had taken Mike's word for the kind of man Jon was. She had put her trust in Mike even though he'd already let her down.

"What are you thinking?" Jon whispered, and she realised that he had drawn her close again, that her hands were resting against his chest, that under her palms she could feel the powerful beating of his heart.

She looked up at him, not sure whether he could see her face clearly enough to read the sincerity in it, not sure whether even now he would be able to trust her. But she had to try.

And maybe then he would be able to tell her about Heather, the girl Shona said he never talked about.

"I was just thinking that maybe it's time we started again," she said quietly. "I was thinking it's time I told you the truth."

Chapter Ten

There was a long silence. Tara heard Jon take a deep breath but other than that he stood quite still. In the fading light she could no longer read his face and there was no way she could tell what his thoughts might be.

"The truth," he said, as if the concept were new to him. "Yes, Tara, I think that would be a very good idea. There have been too many evasions between you and me."

At least he hadn't called them lies, she reflected. But the tone of his voice hadn't helped her at all, and she realised he was going to give no quarter. Until she had given him her truth, Jon wasn't prepared to commit himself in any way. And why should he be?

"So," he said, "what do you have to tell me?"

Tara hesitated, searching for words. Where was she to start? With Mike and the relationship they'd had, which had crumbled so easily? Or with the task Mike had asked her to carry out here in Iceland?

Whatever she decided, it all came back to Mike.

"I don't know quite where to start."

"Why not right here?" Jon suggested and there was a touch of grimness in his tone. "Here in Heklavik. Tell me why you were so keen to come here, Tara."

Tara took a deep breath. Maybe it was the right place to start after all. And she began, hesitantly at first, with that day back in Glasgow when Mike had asked her to visit him and had shown her his computer models of what he expected to happen in Iceland.

"So that's what I wanted to do here," she told Jon. "Have a look at the sites Mike had pinpointed, see what the possibilities were of doing proper tests without alerting anyone, and get an idea of just what the danger would be." She looked up at him, wishing once again that she could read his face in the darkness. "You see, I did tell you the truth. I never wanted to harm Heklavik."

For a few moments, Jon said nothing. Then he asked quietly, "Did Mike ever explain to you why he thought it necessary to be so secretive?"

"Yes, I told you that. Because he didn't think anyone would believe him. He knows how careful you are in Iceland; he didn't think you were likely to welcome a foreigner coming in and telling you your own business. Besides—" she stopped, then went on "—well, I suppose he also wanted the credit of having done all the calculations."

"And did you want that credit too?"

Tara shook her head. "I just wanted to help."

"Help him? Help Mike Redland?"

"No," she said in a low voice. "I wanted to help Iceland." She lifted her face. "I don't have any reason to want to help Mike."

"You haven't told me all of it, have you?" Jon said after another pause. She felt his fingers on her wrists, moving gently in a soft, stroking motion. "You haven't told me what Mike Redland is to you."

"Nothing," she said quickly. "He's nothing to me – *nothing.*"

"But he has been? He was?"

Tara sighed. She might have known that Jon wouldn't let go so easily. "Yes, he was, once. We were engaged – well, not formally but there was a definite understanding. I thought that when I came back from the Antarctic we'd be planning our wedding. Instead—" she heard the quiver in her voice but forced herself to go on, even though the words came through a dry throat "—instead, he was planning a wedding with someone else."

"And did that hurt very much?" Jon asked quietly.

Tara paused. She wanted to say yes, the pain was still with her. But she'd already discovered just what kind of pain that was. "In a way, yes," she said slowly. "But it was my pride that was hurt – I know that now. I just didn't like being rejected!" She glanced up and met his eyes. "I don't think I ever really loved Mike," she said honestly. "He just happened to be around when I needed someone. After that, it became a habit to go around together. And then, somehow, it turned into Mike needing me, but when that happened, I can't say."

"Perhaps it was always so," Jon said. "Some men need women to need them, to make them feel strong. They drain away the woman's strength, but neither of them realises it, and they never understand what's really happening."

Tara shivered. "I think it was like that. That's why Mike was so upset when I went to the Antarctic. It was partly jealousy—"

"And partly because he literally couldn't manage without you. Or without someone – *anyone* – to make him feel big and important in his own eyes." Jon smiled wryly. "People like that never look at themselves through other people's eyes."

Tara gazed at him wonderingly. "How do you know so much?"

"Oh, I don't know much," he said ruefully. "Not much at all. I wish I did." He was silent a moment, then said, "Do you truly think you're over him, Tara? He's been bugging you all this time, hasn't he? Have you finally got him out of your system?"

Tara gazed at him. Did he really not know? Could he

really be unaware that she was committed to him now, whether he wanted her or not? That she would spend the rest of her life loving him, even if it had to be at a distance? She knew again the fear of exposing her feelings. How could she be sure that this new Jon was the real one, that this understanding went deep and true? But she reminded herself that she had to trust him. She had to prove her trust.

"I'm well and truly over him," she said steadily. "I don't really know how I could ever have thought . . . Jon, what is it that people see in each other? I mean, how could anyone prefer Mike Redland to—" She broke off, confused, and then went on bravely "—to someone like you?"

There was a moment of complete silence. Then Jon pulled her roughly towards him. His lips met hers in a bruising kiss and he muttered against her mouth, his words incoherent as lips and tongue tried to manage two tasks at once. Half laughing, half shaken, Tara lifted her face, her lips parted as Jon's kisses rained down. She felt his arms crush her tightly against him and knew that her own arms had wound themselves about his neck, and suddenly it was as if there were no more barriers between them.

But she knew there were still things to be sorted out. Still words to be said, questions to be asked and answered.

"Oh, Tara, Tara," Jon muttered, his lips against her hair. "If you knew what I'd been through . . . Ever since that night when he telephoned you at the hotel, I've wondered if you were pretending it was him when we kissed. Wondered if you were *wishing* it was him . . ."

"Wishing . . . But I—" She shook her head. "Jon, I thought—"

"Well?" His voice was a throaty murmur and he drew her closer against him. "What did you think, Tara, my love?"

It was the second time he had called her that. The first time it seemed to have slipped out by accident. This time she got the distinct impression that he meant it. That he had chosen the phrase deliberately.

"I don't know what I thought now," she whispered. "I seem to have been in such a muddle ever since I came here. Ever since I came back from the Antarctic expedition, really."

"To find Mike engaged to someone else. And I don't suppose you let him know just what you thought of him, did you? I suppose you were 'civilised' about it. Wished them well. Sent them a wedding present."

"As a matter of fact," she confessed, "I went to their wedding."

"You went to their—?" Again, he caught her tightly against him, cradling her in his arms. "Oh Tara, my poor girl! You really did pile the pressure on yourself, didn't you? And you've been doing it ever since. Hiding from your real feelings. Bottling them all up. Going to their wedding, throwing confetti over them, visiting their house, I daresay, even agreeing to do Mike's dirty work for him. No wonder you were ready to take it all out on the first innocent male who came within spitting distance. Not that you ever spat at me," he added thoughtfully, "but I daresay you'd have got around to it."

"And what about you?" she asked softly. "I saw the photograph on your mother's shelf, Jon. The photo of you and Heather. She told me that you would never talk about her. What's that, if it's not hiding from your feelings?" She touched his face with a gentle finger. "Did you know it was Heather that Mike had married, Jon? Can you tell me what happened?"

Can you trust me, she thought, as I've trusted you . . . ?

She looked up into his eyes, knowing that she might be asking too much, that Jon might yet need more patience, more certainty, before he could open up his heart.

For a moment, she thought he wasn't going to answer

178

her. His eyes were hooded, hidden by their lids and the fringe of lashes, his face without expression. She waited, feeling sadly that he was still unsure of her. And then he took a breath, lifted his head and met her gaze.

"My mother didn't tell you anything at all?"

Tara shook her head. "Only that you never spoke about her. But – you looked so happy in the photo . . ." She touched his cheek again. "You don't have to tell me, Jon," she whispered. "You don't have to say anything you don't want to."

He shook his head. "No. You've had the courage to face up to your feelings – I have to do the same." He paused, then went on in a low voice, "I thought we *were* happy, Tara. We'd met a few months earlier in Norway. I'd gone to Oslo as part of a research team and I met Heather there. She was on a trip from university." He paused. "Mike was the leader of the group."

"I remember," Tara said. "It was soon after I'd met Mike myself. I'd have liked to go too, but everything was already arranged." She looked at him, her eyes disturbed. "But he and Heather weren't—"

"Weren't a couple then? No, but I think there had already been a relationship between them. Looking back afterwards, I realised that Heather was definitely in pursuit of him. I just didn't realise it at the time." His mouth twisted a little. "I wasn't particularly perceptive, you see."

"None of us are, when we're in love," Tara said. "That's why—" She broke off and he eyed her quizzically.

"That's why you were afraid to fall in love with me. Because you'd been hurt already."

"Perhaps." She looked up at him again. "What happened?"

"Very little, really. I was dazzled, I suppose. All that blonde glamour. I didn't realise she was simply using me to attract Mike's attention. To make him jealous. I thought she

179

was really and truly in love with me." He laughed without mirth. "In love with *me!* That woman's in love with nobody but herself."

Tara thought of the meal she had eaten with Heather and Mike, the strangely furnished house, the Jane Austen books. None of it, she had suspected at the time, was to Mike's taste. So what was it all about? Was it no more than Heather's desire, her need, to make an impression? A flaunting of her own ego? She'd set out to catch Mike and she'd succeeded. But was it Mike she really wanted or something else? Well, that was their problem, and nothing to do with her or Jon any longer.

Jon was speaking again, his voice flat and toneless.

"We had our wedding planned. Eighteen months ago, it would have been. I'd have been an old married man by now, perhaps with a family starting. And then—" He stopped. "She went back to England to arrange things. We were going to be married there, you see, in her home town. I was starting a new job here, so I couldn't go with her. Besides, there was a lot to do. She wanted the whole thing: bridesmaids, church choir, bells and whistles, the lot. It was going to take a lot of arranging and to tell the truth I wasn't all that thrilled about it. But it was what she wanted, so—" Again, he broke off. "And then she wrote to me and told me it was all off. Said she was sorry – *sorry!* – but the man she really loved had asked her to marry him instead, and of course I couldn't compete with that. Didn't even want to – I'd begun to have doubts myself. So that was that." He shrugged and gave Tara a crooked smile, but his eyes were veiled and she could see that the hurt and anger still simmered inside him.

"If it's any help," she said gently, "I don't think Heather was the girl for you. I've seen her at home. She's all gloss, like a picture in a smart magazine."

"I know. I knew it by then, really. I just didn't want to face the fact that I'd been wrong about her."

"We're all wrong sometimes," Tara said. "I was wrong about Mike. You'd begun to have doubts about Heather. We both had quite a lucky escape, don't you think?"

He looked at her and grinned a little. "You might say so!"

"So what's been bugging us both all this time? Hurt pride?"

He opened his mouth to speak, hesitated, closed it and then gave a sudden shout of laughter and clasped her against him. "Tara, you're marvellous! Yes, that's all it is – just hurt pride. A bruised ego, nothing more. Not wanting to admit I was wrong." He kissed her and said in a wondering tone, "You know, for a long time I thought I'd never love anyone else. I thought I'd never trust anyone else. But now I've met you – *oh, Tara* . . ."

He pulled her close again. His kisses were rough but she received them gladly, knowing that they expressed a depth of feeling he could not communicate in any other way. And knowing too that his love was real, born not of lust nor even desire but of a bond that was already strong and deep, and would grow deeper and stronger for the rest of their lives.

"Tara, Tara," he muttered at last. "If you knew . . . I didn't dare believe it at first. It scared me, the way I felt about you. Yes, I did try to hide it, I tried to pretend it wasn't there. I tried to patronise you, I tried to dislike you, I tried to make *you* dislike *me*—"

"And very nearly succeeded!" Tara told him with a smile.

Jon shuddered and held her close. "Why did I do it? Was I afraid that if I loved you I'd lose you, the way I lost Heather? There's never been anyone since her, Tara. Oh, women, yes, but no one I loved. Not until you."

Tara reached up and drew his head down to hers. She touched his lips with her own, shaping his mouth as he had shaped hers, letting her tongue move in tender exploration.

His body quivered as she pressed against it, and she moved her hands in his hair and over the back of his neck, trying with her body to give him the reassurance he needed, the love he had dared not demand.

"I love you, Jon," she whispered, and then felt the change in him as confidence returned and he touched her with the sureness that had set her afire the night before. Tara closed her eyes as his lips brushed hers very gently, bringing a leaping desire that was like a flame scorching along her nerves and deep into her heart. She gasped, feeling the response that tingled through her blood and prickled her skin, feeling it too in the hardening of his muscles against her melting softness. Inwardly, she exulted. There would be no more hiding of feelings any more, for either of them. From now on their love would be honest, true and open.

And it *was* love. She knew that now, and neither the word nor the idea of it held any more fears for her. The emotion that had been battling for recognition, which they had both tried to ignore and even reject, was able to shine out at last, encompassing them with its glory, like the Northern Lights which had shone above them that first night in the wide valley of Thingvellir.

"Tara," Jon muttered, and his fingers were moving over her body very gently, barely touching her skin and making her want to cry out for more. "Tara, it's going to be all right between us, isn't it? I'm ready for love now, Tara, ready for you." His lips touched hers again, searching, probing, questioning and making statements of their own, statements that needed no words. Tara clung to him, returning kiss for kiss, moulding her body close against him and feeling the heat of desire spread through her entire body.

And then, as he ended the kiss at last, she remembered something and jerked in his arms.

"What is it? Tara, don't pull away from me – not again."

"It's not that. Jon, we've forgotten Heklavik – the volcano, Mike's predictions. We've got to test them. If he's right, there could be an eruption at any time, without any warning." She gazed fearfully towards the mountains that lay in the darkness inland. "We have to decide what to do."

"It's all right," he soothed her. "I tell you, it's all right. Listen to me, Tara." He waited a moment, then said, "Mike's not the only one to have thought of this, you know. We've been working on a similar hypothesis here in Iceland. In fact, it's been one of my projects for quite a while."

Tara stared at him. "*You've* been working on it? But—"

"I've done all the calculations that Mike's done," he said. "And a bit more. Mine have gone further, Tara, and I've carried out some of the tests you say he wants to do. And I don't believe there is any danger."

"But you can't tell! It can be totally unpredictable—"

"Exactly. *Unpredictable.* The pattern that seems to hold doesn't make sense when you take it further, Tara. There might well be an eruption, and it might well happen without warning, but as far as we can tell it's random, Tara. It might just as easily happen in the north. Or the east. Or not at all."

"But it *could* happen?"

"It could happen anywhere, at any time," he said gravely. "And here in Iceland, we live with that possibility. And most of us do survive."

Tara found she had been holding her breath. She let it out in a long sigh. Then Jon spoke again.

"What I'd really like to know is just what Mike's really up to. Why he asked you to come here. Because he must be aware of these results, Tara, and he'd also know that you might not be, having been away for the past year."

"I don't understand," Tara said. "Are you suggesting he had some other reason?"

"And why," Jon continued as if she hadn't spoken, "was he so anxious that I shouldn't find out what he was doing? Because he knew if I did find out, I'd know that he hadn't told you the truth." He looked at her. "Are you sure Mike doesn't have ideas about the holiday business, Tara?"

"*Mike*? No, of course not. He's a geologist. He—" She stopped suddenly. "But *Heather* . . ." Her eyes wide, she stared at him. "Heather's father does. He runs another agency, quite a big one." She remembered Mike's casual questions about her job the night she'd visited them. "Jon, you don't think . . . ?"

"Don't I?" he said grimly. "Don't you? Tara, it's obvious. You go back to him with a comprehensive report on Heklavik, he takes it all in, dismisses all the volcanic material and has a nice factsheet on Heklavik itself, together with all the details about hotels, facilities, location etc—"

"But he could have found all that out for himself, without getting me to do it for him."

"Could he? Without running into me?" Jon shook his head. "He knows I wouldn't trust him an inch, and he knows I have quite a lot of influence. That's why he sent you to do his dirty work."

"And why he told me not to let you know. No wonder you didn't trust me!" Disgust and fury filled Tara. "He nearly ruined everything for us, Jon!"

"Nearly," Jon agreed, and then drew her back into his arms. "But not quite. And now nothing can come between us, can it? Certainly not Mike Redland. Oh, let's forget him." To her relief, she heard the anger replaced by amusement as he said, "It'll be satisfaction enough to know that I've got better taste than him in women. He must have been mad, letting you go!"

He folded his arms about her again and Tara laid her face against his chest, feeling the steady pounding of his heart under her cheek. She had come home at last, after years of wandering in the wilderness. It was almost impossible to believe that she had known Jon less than a week. It was as if they had known each other for ever, had been waiting only to meet.

And we recognised each other at the airport, she thought. We just weren't ready for it then. Or maybe we were scared because we both knew it was the most important thing that was ever going to happen to either of us.

"Tara?" Jon murmured, and she turned her face up for his kiss. And now there was no holding back, no room for thoughts of anything else. Mike, Heather, Alec, all were forgotten in the whirling sensations that tossed her high among the stars, wheeling with the planets, soaring high away from the earthly world into a realm that was made for spirits, where two people could become one and where love surmounted all obstacles.

"We are going to be married, aren't we?" he said against her lips. "As soon as possible?"

"As soon as possible," she agreed, her voice faint with the longings of desire. "But – Jon – I still have to finish the job Alec sent me to do."

"It'll be our honeymoon," he said. "A trip round Iceland together – what could be better?"

Tara laughed. "But I have to go on with the trip *now*, Jon. Winter's coming and much though I enjoy being stranded with you, I think I'd rather get back to a nice comfortable hotel at night. We'll have to wait till I've finished before we can get married."

"So we have the honeymoon first," he said. "Because I'll tell you this, Tara: I'm not letting you out of my sight now. Not for a moment. Not until I'm absolutely sure you're mine."

"I'm yours already," she said softly, and then glanced up. "Jon, look!"

He turned his head and together they stared into the sky.

It was fully dark now, but the deep blue of space was over laid with a display of the Aurora Borealis, lighting the sky with translucent green, royal purple and deep ruby red.

"A midnight rainbow," Jon said softly, and drew Tara close against him. He laid his lips on hers and she closed her eyes. But the beauty of the night was imprinted upon her lids and sounding in her ears. And the heaven they revealed was in her heart.